Mystica - Sunlight and Shadows

Elizabeth Major

Published in 2020 by FeedARead.com Publishing

Copyright © The author as named on the book cover.

First Edition

The author has asserted their moral right under the Copyright, Designs and Patents Act, 1988, to be identified as the author of this work.

All Rights reserved. No part of this publication may be reproduced, copied, stored in a retrieval system, or transmitted, in any form or by any means, without the prior written consent of the copyright holder, nor be otherwise circulated in any form of binding or cover other than that in which it is published and without a similar condition being imposed on the subsequent purchaser.

A CIP catalogue record for this title is available from the British Library.

Contents

Chapter 1	The Beach
Chapter 2	Mystica
Chapter 3	The Baxters
Chapter 4	Philip, Samuel and Henny
Chapter 5	Benedict and Guy
Chapter 6	Mystica
Chapter 7	Philip
Chapter 8	Henny
Chapter 9	Benedict and Guy
Chapter 10	Mystica and the Baxters
Chapter 11	Lucas
Chapter 12	Mystica
Chapter 13	Philip, Brooks and Henny
Chapter 14	Mystica and Benedict
Chapter 15	Lucas and Polly
Chapter 16	Lucas and Edward
Chapter 17	Philip, Henny and Evelyn
Chapter 18	Lizzie
Chapter 19	Mystica, Benedict and Guy
Chapter 20	Edward and Samuel
Chapter 21	Mystica and Benedict
Chapter 22	Brooks, Henny and Ava
Chapter 23	Edward and Henny
Chapter 24	Polly and Phoebe
Chapter 25	Lucas
Chapter 26	Marnie, Joseph and Torrey
Chapter 27	Mystica and Benedict
Chapter 28	Philip and Lizzie
Chapter 29	Samuel and Henny
Chapter 30	Benedict, Samuel and Henny
Chapter 31	Torrey, Henny, Juno, Samuel, and others

Chapter 32	Benedict and Mystica
Chapter 33	Edward, Mystica and Benedict
Chapter 34	Mystica and Philip
Chapter 35	Mystica, Philip and Edward
Chapter 36	Mystica, Benedict, Brooks, Philip and Lizzie
Chapter 37	Seadrift again
Chapter 38	Guy and Edward
Chapter 39	Endings and beginnings

Chapter 1   The Beach

Juno was stomping her way across the sand, kicking it up in gritty clouds. She had removed herself from the small family unit and come out to get some air. Someone had idly suggested that she ought to pin her hair back from her face, instead of allowing it to drape like curtains either side of her ears, shielding her attractive facial features from sight. She quite liked it just the way it was. Besides, Susannah Templeton's hair was like hers, only longer and blonder and Susannah Templeton was older, but not much, and certainly more sophisticated, so she knew a thing or two about style. And you could hardly see her face at all. Not that Juno liked the irritation of hair in her eyes all the time. But it was a bloody cheek, telling her how she should arrange her hair.

"I can't breathe in here, with people telling me what to do all the time," said Juno, and she strutted out, the quintessential drama queen, slamming the door behind her. Fourteen was an awkward age, apparently.

She seemed to strut more often these days than not. Strutting was what she did best.

It annoyed her that she found it hard to pull herself back from being unpleasant. She didn't want to be unpleasant. There was nothing really to be unpleasant about. She was warm, well fed, not overweight, not underweight, more than quite attractive and relatively intelligent with no deep-seated anxieties. Her family loved her; they even quite liked her, most of the time. She loved them too.

So, what was the problem? The problem was that there wasn't really much of a problem. She wanted to shout and lose her temper and nobody gave her any proper justification for doing so. It was so unfair.

She had taken their small terrier, Mouse, a Jack Russell crossed with who-knows-what, and had come down to the beach to settle her mind. Mouse always understood and never made any judgement. Mouse always allowed her to weep salty tears into his ears and sob loudly down his neck when required. He just wagged his tail and licked her face. Mouse was a true friend. Didn't pass judgment. Didn't care what she did with her hair.

Mouse had raced on ahead and was making for the rock pools near the edge of the water. He was looking for small crabs. He had that busy, busy look as he veered sharply from one smell to the next and back again.

Juno continued kicking up sand and calming down.

The wind was getting up and clouds were beginning to form. Juno shivered and watched Mouse who had started yapping and dancing around, the way he always did when she teased him. But she wasn't teasing him this time. He went down on his hunkers and then pranced up; then his head ducked down and he seemed to be pulling at something. Whatever it was, it appeared to be heavy and unyielding.

"Mouse! Mousey! What is it? Here boy!"

Mouse turned and came back in her direction, got halfway and then started to race again to the shore. Juno ran towards him and, as she got nearer, she could see what looked like a bundle of clothing, sodden by the waves.

"Where's all that come from? Nobody can have left their clothes here," she said as she got nearer and then " Bloody hell. Shit and all. It's a person, a body. Mouse, Mousey boy, come here."

She ran up close to where the woman was lying. Juno bent down and knelt in front of this seemingly lifeless form. She immediately started CPR procedures, rhythmically pushing on her chest and was able to detect the flutter of a heartbeat. Had that been there before? Juno didn't know and didn't care. She just went on pressing the chest and then realised that this person was likely to be very cold. She whipped off her jacket and covered the woman's body.

"Mouse, Mouse boy, you must go home. Go home Mousey! Now! Get somebody to come here. Get Dad!"

Mouse looked at her, his head on one side and tail wagging. He went down on his hunkers and yapped a couple of times.

"Oh, come on dog, don't be so bloody stupid! Get Dad. Go home!" she shouted and pointed back up the beach. The dog seemed to have some vague idea that Juno wanted him to leave her. He ran a few steps and then looked back, trying to understand.

"Home, Mouse. Now!"

He was unsettled. She never shouted at him like that. He turned and ran back up the beach. Juno prayed that he was not going to go off and hunt for rabbits. She turned back and kept pumping, and then saw, with some relief, that the woman's chest was starting to move of its own accord with a steady rhythm.

She stirred and Juno moved her head sideways as she spewed out sea water. Her lips were bluish in a dead white face and she was shivering violently.

"Lie still. I'll hold you close, so you get a bit warmer. I don't live far away. The Mouse has gone to fetch help. You'll be OK."

Mouse was confused.

Juno and he always went home together but now there seemed to be an alternative point of interest for her on the beach, and she didn't sound pleased. She had shouted at him and that was unusual. He started off towards home, stopping every now and then to look back towards the beach. In the distance he could see Juno hunched over the large package he had found. That large package seemed to have the scent of a living human, sort of. He could also smell problems though, and danger, and home seemed the right place to be. He continued on his way back to the small unit Juno and her family shared in the village complex.

The complex itself, slightly whimsically named "Seadrift", was well hidden from view. Seadrift had been developed by one of the earliest of the small enlightened groups who had joined together, hidden at first in living quarters down First City secret passageways and dark, concealed alleyways off the central streets in First City, areas where nobody in their right mind would go. There was always the feeling among First City inhabitants that these were the areas populated by a sort of low-life community who possibly scavenged and stole, the only potentially dangerous criminal element that had not been completely eradicated from society. The High Council encouraged this feeling of insecurity and suspicion about these reclusive individuals, to curb the travelling curiosity of the city dwellers, at the same time dismissing them as undesirable, but harmless, souls who were unstable and, fortunately, lived hidden away. They became the forgotten people. The High Council, formed initially to counter catastrophic events, both natural and man-made, were necessarily somewhat autocratic at first, but were trusted to put things right. Somebody had to. Fear bred a blind obedience, which continued even when it started to become apparent that the governing body was corrupt. There was never a moment when the High Council lost confidence in their regime, however, or thought that the First Citizens would seek a life and a world elsewhere, and so any of the initial tight security round the city outskirts was now slipshod and casual.

So, no prying eyes from the High Council would ever have detected the whereabouts of Seadrift and the Seadrifters, unless searching thoroughly and diligently way beyond the outskirts of First City. But then, as High Council dictatorship had become complacent, the members were certain that their rigorous and carefully monitored life arrangements for the citizens were tight and foolproof, and that the citizens' behaviour was, on the whole, totally predictable. No citizen would compromise his position, or isolate himself in such a way as to draw attention to anything irregular. Individual traits and imagination were dealt with rapidly. The Local Observers, spies on their own people, were quick to denounce any of their neighbours who didn't quite toe the line, and nobody was trusted. So nobody rocked the boat.

The High Council had established small catchments, carefully managed by them, at short distances from First City. Travel between the catchments was only undertaken by the High Council and nobody else ever left the confines of their close living and working areas.

The High Council could never have imagined that there were groups of people who had carefully and secretively made their way out of the confines of First City, using old byways long since discarded by the High Council as being beyond repair, too narrow, not efficient enough for High Council official travel. Highways to the catchments were in straight lines like spokes of a wheel from the hub and High Council travellers never saw the need to deviate onto small disused tracks, pointless for their purpose.

The Green Declaration, established in the early days of First City, had been seen as the miracle of salvation, a way forward which would get life back on an even keel, establish some element of restoration to a populace starving for its existence, poisoned by humanity. Firm regulations ensured that nobody ventured even close to the edge of the city, while the large regeneration scheme unfolded beyond. Small sacrifices had to be made in order to preserve the future. And its objectives, though harsh, seemed to be the way forward. Reprisals for failing to follow the regulations were brutal and merciless, so they were generally obeyed through fear and without question. Only hand-picked scientists, known as "The Guardians" worked on the Restoration Plan. Nobody knew exactly what happened beyond the boundaries of the city, where the experimental farming was being undertaken, where the scientists were beavering away for the good of humankind, where the elements of corruption still lodged, however, and the greed of those in power increased as the years went by. Man is, by nature, corrupt and self-seeking; and those holding power were, for the most part, always going to go down that pathway and look for ways to enhance their own lifestyles at the expense of the populace.

In the meantime, citizens in each catchment were encouraged to lead dull, conformist lives; colour had been leached from life and transformed to uniform tones of grey and beige; music and books were banned; learning was done on the basis of what was good for the population to know; suitable males and females were matched and allowed to produce one child. Unsuitable people who showed a spark of something different were considered dangerous; they were sterilised, not allowed to be partnered, and were known as "Loners" and treated with either indifference or vague suspicion.

The Seadrifters had been among those who had broken from this regime. They were a small group, one of several that had formed in silent and careful repudiation of the system and rules created by the High Council. They had made their way to areas beyond First City and its environs, safe in the knowledge that a combination of the complacency of the High Council and their own ability for concealment would allow them to re-form small communities in safety. They were able to establish new beginnings ready for the time when the despotic corrupt regime could be overthrown and a gentle, controlled existence could take its place. They had a heightened awareness of the need for strong control with transparency of government, in order to ensure that the old dishonesty and betrayal would never be repeated. Society would be rebuilt on a foundation of integrity and candour, of trust and honour. Strength had to be demonstrated in ways other than through dishonest autocracy that engendered a harsh regime of fear. But first of all, the cruelty of the present system had to be dealt with and eradicated and a careful regime put in its place that dealt a combination of power and compassion. Dealing with the ordinary people in First City would be like dealing with children let out of school for a joyous holiday full of sunshine. It would need conscious monitoring to ensure they didn't become so over-exuberant that they brought about the disintegration of the very organisation that was there to salvage some dignity and fulfilment to their lives.

Chapter 2   Mystica

Mystica had spent her adult life searching for the beauty and the colour that she knew had once been part of life. A Loner, she had been an outcast in a society full of distrust. Friends were not encouraged, books had been abolished, children were made through computerised partnering, love was not permitted to enter into the equation.

The world had become colourless, filled with a powdery grey gloom, and people were restricted in their day to day living, were discouraged from having friendships and learnt to accept the heaviness of a world with little warmth.

The sky appeared toneless and was filled with slate-grey clouds that caused an almost constant thin drizzle coating the pavements. There was a stale, acrid smell of infertility in the air and an ever-present background hum, distant and mechanical, the sense of an invisible muffled machine, pulsating gently with some anonymous and automatic city life.

The people walking the streets of First City were always silent; they kept their thoughts to themselves, displayed nothing but an air of hopeless futility. They avoided looking at each other. They never spoke. There was a constant air of suspicion.

Thinking back was discouraged and most people had lost the power to remember. But Mystica kept her memories, fuelled by the stories she recalled being told by her grandparents, within the luxury of living alone. She also kept some small coloured treasures that she had been given as a child - a cat in a glass snowstorm dome, some coloured pencils, a faded balloon, a rubber ball and some Indian bells, an apricot silk rose and a pack of playing cards. The cat in the glass dome was standing playing a saxophone in the snowstorm. She called him Tiger, after her grandmother's old cat. For her, he represented love and strength, fidelity and constancy. He was always there when she needed him and if she shook the glass, making the snowflakes whirl around him, he was still there when they subsided and settled, just the same old Tiger. He had become, ridiculously, the most important creature in her life.

But then Mystica met Philip. And Louis. Philip had been partnered with Jo and Louis had been the mandatory single child, the product of that partnership. Louis. He had been the best thing about their coupling, since love was never allowed to enter the partnership equation. Louis kept them in their bond with each other, although there was no emotional intimacy, no real companionship between them.

Jo's "accident" at work was the catalyst for the meeting of two truly matched souls.

Mystica was 39; she had never been allowed the precious gift of motherhood or the opportunity to be partnered. She was designated a Loner. Loners were either viewed with suspicion or disregarded. Mystica kept a low profile in the hope that she would be one of those who was ignored and most of the time her presence was discounted. She had been relegated to the business of living her life alone in a small apartment, no different from any other small apartment, assigned to her by the authorities.

Philip had arrived on her doorstep, with baby Louis, to ask if Mystica could look after him while Philip went to visit Jo in the hospital sector. An immediate bond established itself between the two of them, which grew and surged forward, each time they subsequently met. It was like an electric shock, a shivering steely piercing, a shattering of their lives into a thousand diamond fragments, pushing them towards a sort of fear and an exhilarating joy at the same time. After all, "love" was an emotion and emotions were not permitted - love was a word that had ceased to exist. Besides, Philip was in his mid twenties; it would have seemed an incongruous relationship, with a thirteen year age gap. But the twinning of souls needs no explanation, and an enormous capacity to experience a new and unusual feeling hit them both for the first time; they realised they could interpret this as love.

It became apparent that Jo's accident had been engineered when she had asked too many questions, poked around in too many places and discovered information about the disappearance of her father - information that the High Council had not wanted her to know. The end result, in a short space of time, was her death in the hospital sector, a cold clinical turning off the machine that had pumped blood round her body and kept her vital signs on the edge of life since her admission. Doctors with little imagination and nurses with no compassion just did their job. They were employees of the High Council. Nobody thought of questioning decisions taken by the authorities. It was easier to bury one's head in the sand, get the job done, forget what you thought you might have witnessed.

Mystica and Philip had kept their love under wraps; there was always that strong ever-present feeling of being watched. However much you kept anonymous and in the background, spying was a regular activity, and they knew only too well that there would be someone ready to expose their illicit relationship. They knew that local "Observers" were everywhere and nowhere - you wouldn't know who they were or where they were, or when they might strike, denouncing you to the authorities. The thought of losing each other, and losing such an overwhelming intensity of feeling that went against all the dictats of the regime, was appalling. It became unthinkable, insupportable.

For Mystica, Philip and baby Louis, the turning point came when they found new friends, part of an underground movement formed to shake and unseat the despotic regime that had been set up to implement the Restoration Plan, using the Green Declaration established 30 years before.

Only the "Guardians", handpicked botanists and biological scientists with the highest qualifications, selected from those who obeyed without question, were allowed to work on the Restoration Plan. The High Council established firm regulations and, finally, binding laws that prevented ordinary citizens from leaving the city catchments. Nobody thought of questioning them. After all, nobody was allowed to go hungry, to be unclothed or cold, to be underweight or overweight, so all bodily needs were granted as by right - the same for everyone. It was assumed that the Guardians, of course, were treated the same way. But nobody ever asked, and nobody knew how to check. Thirty years of living in this way had given them a certain feeling of comfort in uniformity.

And then Mystica met a boy called Samuel, a creature of the hidden places, behind the dull grey walls, beyond and beneath the city. Samuel, who had a scarlet handkerchief poking out of his pocket, secured her attention. Colour was not something that was ever apparent in First City and no sensible, anonymous citizen would draw attention to themselves by sporting anything so bright. He smiled at her as she walked past him. Samuel was part of a small group, a covert circle of warm and loving people who had found a way to enjoy the sun again. Hidden away from the rest of the community, they had managed to live a parallel existence; their lives were successfully concealed from the High Council, because of the administration's careless sense of security, their inaccurate feeling of confidence in an increasingly unstable stability. This group had succeeded in diverting the governing body's resources, subtly and by small degrees, through spurs to the energy lines and pipes, unnoticed and unconsidered through the arrogance of the High Council, an organisation that had been all-powerful for so long that notions of its own infallibility were never questioned.

When it became inevitable that the safety of Mystica and Philip was likely to be in danger, they were encouraged by Samuel to take shelter with this group. Here, for the first time, they felt safe and nourished and they experienced the warmth and love of a community at peace with itself. An irrepressible young girl, Henny, was attracted to Philip and flirted with him outrageously. He had never been exposed to anything quite like that before and found it flattering but not easy to handle. For the first time there were feelings of uncertainty, jealousy and naivety for both Mystica and Philip, but the wisdom of Edward, the octogenarian leader of the community, put things into some sort of context that made it more comfortable for them both. Philip knew that his love for Mystica was infinite, and Henny was wide open with her declaration that Samuel was really the one she was setting her sights on, but she was outrageously flirtatious with every man she came in contact with. Edward had made it clear that he thought that Mystica and Philip, and indeed baby Louis, would be a great asset and the group's aspirations would be achieved with their help. He felt, however, that they should have some time away from the main community, in one of the smaller splinter groups some distance from First City, to enjoy the experience of living as a small loving family of three. After all, a relationship founded on deep love was new to them both.

The carefree journey to the outer territory, down overgrown pathways and across rough terrain, was undertaken with suppressed excitement, confidence and joy, until Mystica realised that her beloved Tiger, her cat in a snowstorm, had been left behind. Philip insisted on going back for it. Mystica had an instant childlike reaction, a feeling of delight that he thought enough of her to return for one of the possessions she held dear. It was naive and, she realised as soon as he was out of sight, that it was stupid and dangerous for him to return and for them to be separated.

As Philip carefully approached the outer limits of First City again, he had not noticed Henny, lurking in the shadows, as she often did in order to check on the comings and goings of strangers who might prove unsafe and put their community in danger. She watched him and was horrified to see him being led towards the darkness of the high city walls by Lucas, one of Mystica's erstwhile neighbours. Lucas was known to be married to a Local Observer, an unpleasant and ruthless woman who had little thought for anyone but a great deal of interest in her own advancement within the regime. Lucas was desperate. He had seen Philip and pulled him into the shadows while he explained that he was, himself, seeking a new life outside the regime. Henny, knowing only what she saw from the distant shadows, assumed that Philip had been caught and taken into custody by Lucas for questioning by the authorities. Horrified by what she thought was the end of the road for Philip, she made the decision to strike out on her own and look for Mystica.

She left a note for Samuel in a hidden mail box and having some vague idea of the direction in which Philip and Mystica had gone, she eventually found her way into the fringes of the forest region.

She had made several small secretive forays down these untrodden tracks in the past, as a sense of adventure was in her blood, but she had never gone too far. She had always kept sight of the outer limits of First City in the distance before. After several hours, exhausted and emotionally drained, Henny at last found Mystica who was surprised to see her instead of Philip. Henny told her what she had witnessed. She explained that she had seen Lucas pull Philip into the shadows. She left Mystica to come to her own conclusions. The tale, however, had seemed to magnify and change slightly, on her journey, so that according to Henny some considerable force had been used. It seemed as if everything had gone badly wrong.

Mystica shook her head. This couldn't be true. Henny looked away and Mystica sank down to the ground. She looked up and fixed her eyes on Henny. This must be wrong, surely. Her eyes pleaded silently for Henny to tell her this was wrong. But then, if Philip were alright it would have been him standing there, not Henny. Philip. Not Henny.

"No!" she shouted and her face crumpled in an agony of sadness. Suddenly her happiness had come crashing down. She stood up quickly, turned and ran further into the woods, blind to direction. In a matter of seconds the dark trees had swallowed her up and, in the obscurity of the trees, Henny could no longer see which way she had gone.

"Stop! Wait! Mystica, don't. We have to go back. It's not safe and you'll make mistakes on your own. Don't go further, please. I've come to help you! Please wait!"

Henny stared into the deepening gloom but she couldn't see Mystica, and the more she stared the less she could tell the direction that Mystica had taken. The trees all looked much the same and panic made her even less able to work out the path Mystica had rushed along. Henny suddenly felt lost and frightened. She cried large wailing sobs like the child she still undoubtedly was. Being quite alone, she didn't know what to do for the best. Slowly she turned and went back the way she had come. There was, anyway, the feeling that she, still a child in reality, was trying to deal with an impossible situation. She needed help.

Meanwhile, Mystica ran on blindly, not caring where she was going; she was aware only of the need to put distance between herself and the unacceptable. There was a large, silent scream deep inside her throat and she felt as if her soul had shattered. She raced on, further into the shade until she eventually tripped over a fallen branch and fell face downwards onto a bed of pine needles. She lay panting, in a state of near collapse, and then allowed herself to shed the tears that had been waiting. She sobbed convulsively and the paroxysms of pain and grief raged until she could cry no more. She whimpered and, drawing her knees up to her chest, covered her head with her arms. Without Philip and Louis there was no meaning to her life any more.

She got up and stumbled on. Coming through the forest darkness, she saw a pinhole of bright light that got larger as she approached the edge of the trees. She heard the sounds of water, of waves lapping on a shoreline. She had reached a sea estuary that was flashed across with golden sunlight, with a lustrous intensity. The brightness scorched across her face and she shielded her eyes until she got used to the light. The magnitude of this potent warmth, this brilliance and energy, filled her with the deepest and most agonising sorrow she had ever experienced. It burned into her chest and she felt she could hardly breathe. This was what she had been seeking - her rainbow - and she would no longer be able to share this promise of colour and light with the two people she loved.

Mystica found her hands shaking and her body shivered violently against the heat of the sun. She moved slowly towards the stretch of a wide sandy beach, past the grasses and weeds on the edges of some sand dunes that lay at the edge of the forest she had trawled through. From pictures in her grandfather's old natural history books, she recognised insipid green goosefoot and the tall upright shoots of sea beet, an occasional marsh dock, when the ground thinned out, and the yellow-grey of sea sandwort. Sharp spikes of grass stood proud in the dunes like thin, green whips that laced and whipped into Mystica's legs as she trudged through the shifting sand. Up the high sides, she plugged her feet deep in the bleached rock dust and skimmed down through the undulating hills, showering the grains and feeling the grittiness in her eyes and teeth, until she stopped at the top of the dunes, looking towards the edge of the beach. The wind threw the soft and drifting sand into her face in an arbitrary fashion. She couldn't see where she was going any more. Her cheeks burned and her eyes stung as the sand clogged her tears.

She no longer cared. She had no wish to be part of a life without Philip and Louis.

She moved from the dunes to where the sand was firmer and damp. Turning to face the water, Mystica walked with determined strides down the beach, discarding her small pool of possessions as she went, kicking at small hillocks of sand, towards the shoreline, into the waves. Continuing into the sharp shock coldness of the water, she felt herself buffeted by the breakers, but pushed her way deeper and deeper into the sea, the roar and crash of each breaking wave cracking across her body, stinging her skin. She had lost Philip and Louis. Their lives had been re-gained by the system. First City, the authorities, the High Council had won again. What had she to live for?

She waded on, forcing a path through the waves, her face upturned to the golden shimmer of the sun, until the water covered her, the waves burst like thunder in her ears and her body seemed to shatter with the inflow of the ocean. She realised that this was a final step. There was nothing beyond this. She could go silently and rapidly, quietly disappearing beneath the surface. She felt separate from the water, her mind started to become numb and memories faded as a strange calmness settled over her. It would soon be finished. She knew that, if she allowed the water to surge into her lungs, she would drift away.

Or she could survive.

Her body was buffeted by the surging waves, and her head surfaced above them as the sharpness of the water sliced into her and took her by surprise. Like a rough serrated knife blade, the full impact of what was happening suddenly stabbed at her and she had an overwhelming desire to live, not to give up. Her mind cleared and, in that moment of clarity, she thought that perhaps Philip and Louis would be safe, perhaps she could go back and find them; the possibility was faint and feeble, but it pulsed at the back of her mind.

Above all, she experienced a sudden determination not to sacrifice herself to the sea. She had found normality in her life with Philip and Louis and then with Edward and Samuel and the closely hidden secretive community that lay beyond the confines of First City. Even the remotest chance of being with them again gave her the frantic wish to survive.

The strong current in the estuary carried her up and away from the open sea. She was held in its pull and her body was dragged relentlessly through the water. She felt cold and exhausted. The waves continued to pound across her and somehow her head remained above the water line. It was as if she was being lifted or driven gently through the water. She thought she could feel something against her abdomen, supporting her in some way. She was pulled further up the estuary, sucked into the intensity of the tidal power, propelled away from where she had first entered the water. The breakers then became overwhelming and she felt herself powerless as each gigantic wave crashed into her. She gave in to the force of the sea and, as she was hurled onto the shoreline, she remembered no more.

Chapter 3   The Baxters

Torrey Baxter and his parents were still sitting round the table, the remnants of their meal waiting to be cleared. His mother, Marnie, was sitting back enjoying a third glass of wine and his father was finishing off the last bit of a rather excellent apple pie.

"My mother always made a good apple pie," Joseph Baxter reminisced. "I made the right decision falling for you, didn't I? This is almost as good as hers."

Marnie batted him with a table mat.

"And you, Joseph, are almost as cheeky as your father was," she said.

She sighed. "I love these summer evenings when the sun does its bit on the water and makes us all glad to be alive. Even Juno likes it, in spite of her fourteen year old dismissal of everything around her. I suppose she'll grow out of it."

"I did," said the sixteen year old Torrey. "She's just a child. She'll grow up in a year or so."

"Such wise words from such an old man," Joseph teased. "Still, I guess she could do with a few more companions of her own age. I suppose we have cut ourselves off a bit, in this outpost. There's nobody for her really."

"Rubbish," said Marnie. "There are four more families here in the community and each of them has a child about Juno's age."

"Mmm. Charlie Lewis? Spotty and immature. I don't think so. Susannah Templeton? Well, she is a good twelve months or so older than Juno and a potentially evil influence on her."

"Oh, I don't know," protested Torrey. "She's good fun."

"Yes. That's just what I mean," said his father. "She is full of the most extraordinarily foul language I've ever heard, and that's bearing in mind my great-grandfather was a sailor, so it isn't as if I haven't heard it all before."

"Oh Joseph, you are an old stick-in-the-mud," laughed Marnie. "She's alright, and you never met your great-grandfather. But I don't think Juno has much time for Susannah."

"Oh I wouldn't be too sure of that," said Joseph "Susannah seems to be a role model of sorts, as far as I can see."

"Susannah likes to impress and Juno is impressionable, but Mum's right. She doesn't hang out with Susannah much really. Not her type at all, not deep down. Of course, there's always Guy Eastman," said Torrey. "He's more Juno's style. A bit boring I think, but he's alright I guess."

Joseph nodded. "Guy's a nice lad. And, of all of them, he's the one Juno has most time for. But I still think she'd rather play with that dog, than deal with humans."

Right on cue, Mouse got to the door of the family home and scratched at the grass-covered wood. He started to make squeaking noises and then scratched at the door again.

"He's raced her home," said Joseph. "Torrey, let him in before he scratches the door to pieces."

Torrey pressed a button on the wall and the door slid upwards and seemed to disappear into the hillside. Mouse ran into the family room, looking bewildered and rushed from one to another, finishing off with Joseph. He sat staring up at Joseph and then barked. Now, Mouse wasn't a barkative dog. He barked if strangers approached the house. He barked with exuberance when he realised he was going out for a walk along the beach with Juno. But he never barked on returning from a walk.

"Where's that girl, Mouse? Where's Juno got to, eh?" Joseph patted the dog and playfully tickled him behind the ears.

Mouse got up again and circled the family table, racing back to stand in front of Joseph, barking again. It sounded slightly hysterical, Joseph thought, and he went over to the door and looked out.

"Juno," he called. "Juno, come on. Your dog's going crazy here. Come and calm him down and then we can shut the door. It's draughty!"

He looked out, but Juno was not in sight.

Mouse rushed towards the door, still barking, and it was such an unusual situation, with Juno nowhere to be seen, that Joseph thought he should perhaps investigate further.

"Mouse, be quiet!" Joseph shouted. "I can't hear myself think."

But Mouse kept on.

"Torrey, perhaps you and I ought to do down towards the beach and just check that Juno hasn't done something daft."

"What do you mean?" said Marnie anxiously.

"Well, she may have fallen and twisted her ankle. You know how she skips over those jagged rock pools. Our young mountain goat might just have stumbled. Torrey and I will take a look."

The two of them set off, with Mouse excitedly yapping round them, racing ahead and then rushing back.

"I must say, I've never seen the dog quite like this before," said Joseph.

Mouse ran on ahead and kept coming back and barking again, checking that they were still there following him. When they reached the dunes, Torrey ran on ahead. At the top of the dunes he turned back towards his father.

"She's there!" he shouted, "Down the beach a bit, kneeling by something. Don't know what. Hey Juno, what's up?"

Juno remained kneeling by Mystica.

"You'll be OK now," she said. "It's my Dad and my brother. Hang in there. We'll get you home. You're safe now."

She kept rubbing Mystica's arms and turned towards Torrey.

"Hurry up," she shouted. "I've got a shipwrecked sailor here."

Torrey ran down the beach, followed closely by his father. Mouse was sidetracked and went off to investigate a small rock pool. The sand was smooth and dry, but the tide was coming in fast and soon would be close to where Juno was tending Mystica.

"God, Juno!" exclaimed Torrey. "Where did you find her?"

Juno shot him a withering glance.

"Hell's teeth, Torrey! I found her under a mussel shell, idiot!" Mystica stirred and moaned.

"Come on, young lady" said Joseph. "We'll soon have you home in the warm. Torrey, give me a hand. We'll support her between us. Juno, run on ahead and get your mother to have something warm, soup or hot tea - anything to help warm this poor creature up. A nip of brandy might help as well, for me if not her."

Juno raced on towards their home, Mouse running at her heels, still full of excitement. Marnie was waiting anxiously by the open door as Juno charged in, out of breath and flushed.

"Dad says to have something hot, soup or tea or anything. Mouse and I found a woman washed up on the beach. She's alive. I did some CPR and she started to breathe properly, but she's poorly."

"I thought something had happened to you, when Mouse came back so excited," said her mother. "I've never seen the dog in such a state."

"Me? Hell, no," replied Juno. "I'm fine, but this lady might need a bit of looking after. Wow, good old Mouse! I didn't know if he would really do what I needed him to do, but he's a star."

"Fetch some dry warm clothes, will you Juno love? Something you think might fit her."

Juno disappeared without a word and came back with some towels as well.

"Good thinking, love. I guess she'll still be pretty wet."

Marnie put the kettle on to boil, fetched some heated body pads to warm up in an ancient microwave and fetched a frozen soup capsule which she placed in a container and switched a button at the side. Instantly there was the aroma of warm nourishing lentils and tomatoes. Everything was prepared by the time Joseph and Torrey carried Mystica gently into the house.

"Put her on the futon by the fire," said Marnie. "Poor girl. I wonder what on earth happened. Where's she come from? We don't exactly have a tourist industry round here."

"All in good time," replied Joseph. "Let's get her back in the land of the living properly first. Torrey, bank the fire up will you.

Please? Then you and I had better leave the ladies alone to sort out our visitor."

Joseph pulled the futon nearer the fire as Torrey threw on a couple of logs which spat and crackled and shot flames up the chimney. The noise made Mystica stir again. She could already start to feel life pulsing back into her. Her bones were warming up and she opened her eyes.

"Thank you. I don't...I can't think...where?"

"Hush, all in good time" said Marnie. "You're alive! And you're safe. That's what matters. Juno and I will help you out of those wet things. There's some soup on the go and some heated pads to make sure your body is really back to its proper temperature. You men, make sure the spare bed in Juno's room has clean sheets and a heated bedding pad."

Joseph and Torrey left the room and tramped down a carved wooden staircase, which creaked a little.

The Baxters' home unit was built in the woods beyond the sand dunes. It was partly below ground and rose in a gentle slope upwards with a steeper section which housed the hidden doorway. A green sward covered its roof, partially camouflaging the structure from the outside world. It was one of seven units all within an area of about a mile and cultivated fields stretched behind, with food processing areas below ground for safety but with natural light filtered in and concentrated with maximum storage potential for newly harvested crops in the best possible conditions. Joseph was the overall manager of the plant and the seven families nearby each contributed in their own way to the lifestyle they had selected, away from First City, a million miles from the concepts developed by the High Council. This was a community based on a benign collectivism, a growing simple scheme to ensure that everybody's skills were of use and each person contributed to the welfare of the whole. Not a new idea by any means, but way beyond the comprehension now of the sad inhabitants of First City, where the citizens just spent any time away from work minding their own business and ensuring that they operated as anonymous individuals, as grey and uninteresting as the sky.

Joseph and Torrey pulled the extra bed from its wall moorings and made it up with a soft mattress, sheets and covers, plus a bed pad which infused the whole with a pinkish glow and a healthy warmth. They went back downstairs and Mystica was dry and dressed in clean clothes, a mixture of styles selected by Juno. She was sitting by the fire and the pallor of her face was slowly receding, although she was visibly shaking.

"Should I go and fetch Benedict Eastman?" asked Torrey.

"Well yes, I guess it might be sensible for someone with a medical eye to take a look at this young lady," Joseph replied. "Yes, nip over to the Eastmans' please Torrey, but I think we should keep our visitor's arrival under wraps for a while."

"I'm...so...sorry," mumbled Mystica. "I'm... putting you... to a lot of trouble." Her voice came in a half whisper and her throat hurt.

"It's no trouble at all," said Marnie. "We don't get many visitors, as you might imagine."

"None really. 'specially not straight out of the sea!" Juno smiled at Mystica and held out the bowl of soup. "Here, I'll hold this for you. Just dip in with the spoon. It might be easier."

Mystica took the small spoon gratefully and dipped it into the bowl. The sudden warmth of the soup surprised her and caught at the back of her throat, making her splutter and cough. She put her hand up to her mouth instinctively to stop any liquid escaping. Her hand was shaking with cold. Marnie came forward gently and gave her a tissue. She smiled with gratitude and shook her head apologetically.

"Don't worry," Marnie said quietly. "Take your time. I'm sure it can't help, having us all sitting round watching you. Juno, love, Mousie hasn't been fed yet. I'll hold the soup bowl. Could you please...?

"Oh my poor little Mouse bird!" said Juno."We forgot about you. And you're a hero! Come on, let's see what we've got for you. Come on Mouse, good boy!"

Mouse wagged his tail expectantly, and ran round in a circle, as Juno jumped up and walked over to his food dish. She clapped her hands at him and he followed close on her heels, taking little excited jumps in mid-air.

Joseph sat down and helped himself to another glass of wine. Marnie looked at him quizzically.

"What?" he asked. "Did you want another one Marnie, my little vin rouge flower?"

Marnie smiled and held out her glass.

"And perhaps our visitor?" she said.

"Perhaps we had better wait until Ben's been and given the all clear," said Joseph, but refilled Marnie's glass.

Mystica had almost finished the soup when the door opened and in came Torrey, followed by a tall man in his early forties. Benedict Eastman was slim and athletic-looking. He had a face that looked as if it had seen some interesting and maybe harrowing things in its time, a lived-in comfortable face, with some lines of compassion etched in, fringed with the remembrance of difficult experiences. He drew up a chair next to Mystica and smiled at her.

"Hello Joseph, Marnie. Hi Juno. Well, what - or who - have we here?" he said. He put his hand up palm facing her, as she struggled to say something. "No, don't answer that yet. Plenty of time to hear your story. Let's just take a look at you first."

Marnie asked if they should leave him with Mystica, but he shook his head.

"No need," he said. "I shall do one or two tests but you can stay. There's obviously been a small element of potential hypothermia, but it's been caught early and the warming up has been gradual but steady I would say. I want to check for any renal and lung problems, test her blood and cardiac responses and so on. Juno, how long did you need to do CPR? How long before she responded?"

"Very quickly, I'd say, within a few seconds really, but I don't know how long she'd been on the beach. She was on the shoreline but I think she'd only been there a very short time; the tide had pushed her in and was on the turn. Mouse saw her first and I saw her pretty soon after that as I wanted to know what he was barking at. I wrapped her in my coat and sent Mouse home to fetch Dad. She coughed up water and stuff and then I just tried to keep her warm until Dad and Torrey came."

Benedict stuck a recovery patch on to Mystica's arm. It was the size of a small coin and paper thin.

"That will help," he said. "Leave it on for 24 hours if possible. You did well, Juno. There might have been a very different picture if you hadn't come on the scene and started to work on her as soon as you did. I'd say you probably saved this young lady's life."

Mystica half smiled as she realised that this was the second time she had been referred to as a 'young lady'. She, at 39, had felt the onslaught of middle-age for a few years. How ridiculous that she should think of this at a time when her very existence had been in question. But then, maybe it is at these times of threat that small things start to become important and perhaps it was a good thing that a spot of vanity should be allowed to creep in. It was a comfort suddenly to be thought of as a 'young lady', although a near brush with death made her feel as vulnerable as a young child.

Ben Eastman finished his examination and accepted a glass of wine. He sat looking at Mystica, a warm smile wrinkling up his eyes.

She looked back at him, and around at the family, her face displaying her gratitude. For the most part she had stopped shaking and the warmth of the soup, the fire and the people had started to seep through to her bones and her soul.

"Thank you," she said. "Thank you all. My name is ... I must explain... Myst... I don't quite know..."

Mystica couldn't remember her name properly. She was taken aback to realise that there appeared to be a large gap in her memory, an empty space where her name ought to be, and the more she fought to remember the more the faint memory of a name slipped away.

"Well yes, a bit of a mystery indeed. I, for one, will be most interested to hear how you arrived on our beach," said Ben Eastman. "But there's no rush. If it's alright with you, Marnie, I think our guest should stay with you. She needs quiet and rest for a few days."

"Yes, of course," said Marnie straight away. "We never have visitors, so it will be a treat."

"She is going to be fine, thanks to Mouse, and Juno in particular, but it's early days yet and there still could be a complication or two."

"I have no clothes, no belongings," said Mystica. "Just what I almost gave to the sea."

"Don't worry about anything. Juno and I can kit you out with things to wear. They may not be quite your cup of tea, but I think we're all about the same size. Juno's things might be a bit bizarre, but it'll give her an excuse to find new items. We make our own clothes mainly, or rely on more experienced dressmakers here at Seadrift, especially in my case. I'm no seamstress."

"I'd be grateful for anything that covers me up and keeps me warm and if that gives Juno the opportunity to replenish her wardrobe, then I shall be delighted."

Ben smiled at Mystica. "And we'll all need to keep an eye on you, just for a while."

"Thank you...Dr?"

"My name's Benedict Eastman. Ben. Marnie and Juno, could you help this young lady to her bed now? I think rest is what she needs and I know you will have warmed the bed first. She needs to be kept in an even temperature as her body recovers from the shock, and a bit of a battering I would say. I'll look in tomorrow morning and see how things are."

Marnie and Juno helped Mystica to her feet. She was unsteady and trembling, but found she could walk with their help.

"You'll be sharing with me," said Juno. "Hope that's OK?"

Mystica smiled and nodded. "Perfect," she said.

Joseph walked to the entrance with Ben.

"Will she be OK really?" he asked.

"Of course," said Ben. "But I'm interested to hear how she came to be in the water in the first place. We never have visitors and that was certainly an extraordinary way to arrive. There's a bit of a story there I think. My feeling is that her physical recovery will be swift, but I think there may be some emotional hurdle that she needs to clear that will take time and understanding. I wish my Ellie were still here. She would have been wonderful - a great counsellor was Ellie. She listened and helped hundreds of lost and losing souls, bruised by the regime and by their own helplessness."

Joseph gripped Benedict's arm and nodded at him. Ben managed a faint smile.

"She just wasn't able to help herself."

Chapter 4   Philip, Samuel and Henny

Henny had found her way back to the fringes of First City and met Philip and Samuel. Henny had been missing for longer than usual and they had found her note explaining that she had gone to find Mystica. They had set out to follow her.

Henny was astonished to find Philip, and then horrified when she realised how she had jumped to the wrong conclusions about his meeting with Lucas. She burst into noisy tears and eventually admitted what she had done, but it was not the time for recriminations.

They moved cautiously towards the outer regions beyond First City; here, very occasionally, there were people watching and waiting, ready to stop anyone with the temerity to think that they could leave the catchment. They continued the journey swiftly, along the overgrown tracks, through weeds and long grasses, Philip almost running, covering the ground in anxious strides. Samuel and Henny followed on. Philip knew the way, but it was a couple of hours before they reached the point at which he had left Mystica, in the relative safety of the forest.

Of course, she was nowhere to be seen, but he saw the pine needles that had been trampled underfoot as she had lunged out of the darkness of the trees and, more slowly, he followed the trail. Henny realised that she should have done this.

"I should have found her," she said. "I should never have just left, but I panicked. I just couldn't think what best to do."

Samuel sighed. "With hindsight we might all do things differently. You were sensible to come back for us. It won't help to torture yourself with the thought of what other measures you could have taken. Let's just find her now."

Philip, Samuel and Henny pushed their way through the forest, seeing a glimmer of bright light through the trees, getting ever larger. Philip felt a mixture of hope and sagging inevitability that burrowed deep into his soul. He knew what he wanted so much to find. He knew what he dreaded would be there.

The sun was blinding as they arrived at the beach full of tinted warm specks among the pale sand of the western coast, nestling between the neutral stones, beside the shining sea. They saw the abandonment of old deckchairs, gloriously multicoloured, planted along the edge of the beach and seeping into the dunes. Here was a forgotten piece left alone, allowed to be, a freak of time.

And there, on the sand, lay Mystica's bag of treasures, with a set of footsteps down towards the water's edge. Philip knelt down and tipped out the contents of the bag. There was the apricot rose and the lavender bag, the rubber ball and the Kingfisher cards. Philip stood up and followed the line of footsteps to the water's edge, hesitatingly at first and then he gathered speed and ran headlong towards the shore, uttering a tormented and heart-wrenching cry. He searched the shoreline frantically, wading into the water and then returning. At last he sank down into the wet sand at the water's edge and stared out to the horizon, his face tormented with grief.

Henny was frightened. She had never experienced such desolation and sorrow. She looked at Samuel; his face echoed her misery. He caught her hand and together they walked down to Philip and drew him up to his feet.

"I want to be with her," shouted Philip.

"And Louis?" questioned Samuel gently.

Philip looked at him and wept. Slowly the three of them walked back up the beach.

At the edge of the dunes Philip knelt again and picked up the apricot rose and the lavender bag.

"This was so much what she had been seeking. Mystica's rainbow world of colour," he said. "I can't believe that she could have just walked away into the sea."

He turned round and looked again towards the shoreline, seeing the waves dancing in their innocence. He scoured the beach, shielding his eyes from the sun, looking for a sign that Mystica's footsteps angled away from the water's edge, but the footsteps ceased and there were no further marks in the sand; the tide had gone out and the surface was left with a sudden ghostliness where the track ended. He collected the rubber ball, still a piercing shiny blue, and the Kingfisher playing cards and put them slowly back in to Mystica's bag. He picked the bag up, held it to his face and breathed deeply, inhaling the memory of her skin.

"I don't want to leave," he said. "I can't go. She could be here somewhere. I'm not going. I must stay, just in case..."

"Philip, we have to go," replied Samuel. "You have a little boy waiting for you. Louis will be bewildered by the last few hours. He will need you. And you will very much need him. I...I'm not sure how safe it is for any of us here. We don't know how far the Guardians post their observation groups. It's probably OK, but I just don't know. We shouldn't be out in the open for too long."

Samuel tucked his arm in Philip's and firmly steered him back towards the pine forest. It was a slow journey. Philip kept looking behind him to the sea, staring at the horizon, looking up to the sky and round towards the hills and the sand dunes that edged the beach. Just in case.

The journey back to First City was silent. A forlorn little group returned to the community, keeping close to the walls, where the shadows were deep. Edward was there waiting to greet them, with a small group of friends. He took one look at their faces and the fact that Mystica wasn't with them told its own story. He gently hugged Philip and led him away from the rest of the group.

Chapter 5   Benedict and Guy

When Benedict arrived home, he activated the door remotely and it slid open, seeming to disappear into the hillside.

"What was all that about?" asked his son. "I had a message from Juno about a woman washed up on the beach. Is that right?" Ben didn't say anything. He went over to the kitchen area and poured himself a large glass of iced orange juice from the dispenser. He sat down heavily and turned the glass slowly in his hands. He held it up to the light.

"I think the orange content is low. It seems weak and doesn't really hit the spot. We need to upgrade the plant system. Remind me to let Joseph know later."

"Dad! What happened? And how did it happen? This is the first exciting thing that seems to have arrived on our doorstep since we left First City and you talk about the juicing system! Tell me," said Guy.

"It's a bit of a mystery. We don't know anything about her, not even her name. I promise you. I'm as intrigued as you are. All I can say is that she's going to be alright. It could have been a pretty close call, but she'll be fine" replied Ben.

"I might find out a bit more tomorrow. I'll need to go back and check on her."

"Can I come too?" asked Guy.

"I think not, not yet. Let's give her a bit of space," replied Ben. "You are right - these events don't happen on our doorstep and I think she needs time to recover from something other than a near drowning."

Guy had saved the remnants of a meal for his father and they sat in companionable silence for a while, as Benedict finished off a lukewarm dish of rather glutinous macaroni cheese.

"Sorry. I should have kept it in the heat maintainer. Didn't think you'd be as long. Sorry. I can't really cook. I know that nothing tastes as good as it used to..." Guy trailed off and looked down at the floor.

Benedict put his fork down and took hold of the boy's hands.

"When your mother was taken, it was the worst day of my life," he said. "We must have been the only really successful partnering in the history of First City. Our love blossomed and grew, despite the regime and its determination to ensure that partners were devoid of emotion or feeling of any kind for each other. When you love as fiercely as we did, it is impossible to disguise it."

Ben felt Guy squeeze his hands.

"Ellie had tenderness," he went on, "a wonderful sense of understanding for others, and an astonishing ability to listen and advise. These qualities led her to question the way things were done by the authorities and so she was silenced. She was there one day, when I left for the Health Sector. I collected you from the nursery after the clinic session and when we returned home, our living area was empty. She had vanished. You were too young to understand, although you felt her loss as any baby would. In the middle of your own desolation, you instinctively knew my misery and became my biggest comfort. Ellie was the first best thing that had ever happened to me. You were the next and it's no exaggeration to say that you saved me, kept me going, preserved my sanity and loved me unconditionally through all my moments of despair. I guess young children have an instinct for what is required sometimes and, of course, you had inherited so much of your mother's compassion that your instincts were finely tuned already. I have been the luckiest of fathers."

"Dad, I wish I'd had time to get to know her. Did you ever find out what had happened?"

"No. The authorities were wonderful at closing ranks and maintaining a tight silence, and my hands were tied. I couldn't delve too deeply without being in danger of losing you too."

"I think I remember her and I think I remember things, small things, a sort of warm feeling, a certain smell."

"I know just what you mean," said Ben, "and I can still hear her voice as well." He coughed and put the back of his hand up to his lips.

"But, you're right," he said, standing up. "You're no cook."

"Dad, what was First City like and why did we move?"

"I met a man called Edward, a wise individual who had been one of the prime movers in the early part of the Restoration Plan. He was part of the High Council."

"The High Council? What was this all about? God, Dad I haven't heard about any of this! How is it that I'm only hearing about it now?"

"I heard about it when I was your age, as did my parents. It was made clear to me that young children only need to know the simplest bits of information, 'undecorated' if you like."

"So why are we here? What is that High Council thing?"

"The ruling organisation you might call it. The members started off with the best of intentions I suppose, to counteract some pretty awful happenings. Democracy had been tried and found wanting, although it was the closest to a fair regime, even with all the problems. But gradually and inevitably, greed stepped in and, although certain improvements were put in place, there were strong and ruthless characters who saw an opportunity for personal gain. The Green Declaration, devised to control the system and get things back on an even keel, became used for dictatorial purposes. Rules were put in place as to how one should live, in order to improve the long-term survival of the human race. These rules were more for the benefit of the governing class than the future of humanity. They were stringent, cruel and dangerous, and punishment for those who failed to obey was swift and merciless. But you only knew about this by hearsay. People were not punished openly and transparently. They were just removed from society."

"Like my mother?"

"Like your lovely mother. We never saw them again."

"It sounds bloody awful, but then what?"

" There were government spies - Local Observers they were called - and they reported back to the authorities and kept a close eye on people who were seen to be "different", to be a potential threat to the norm."

"So what about Edward, this chap you met? What happened to him? It doesn't sound as if he was removed."

"Edward saw what was going on and decided that he had to try and repair the new damage that was being done, to counteract the new catastrophe. He realised that he had to build up some sort of counter-group, apart from the authorities, away from the regime. So he removed himself and gathered together a small company of sympathetic like-minded people with scruples and the ability to remain silent. They slipped into the shadows and established a hidden "village" within the thick walls and dark passages of the edge of First City. Edward found me when I was in my greatest need of human comfort and when I needed help for you too. I went to stay with him and his group in their covert hideaway. He is a great mender of human souls. I escaped the horror and I spent some time with you in the community learning how to avoid hate, how to harness any talents or skills I possessed and, I hope, how to embrace humility. It took a while. "

Benedict helped himself to a large brandy, poured into a pre-warmed glass, at just the right temperature. He took a swig and sighed with a sort of contentment as the warmth comforted him. He and Guy had never discussed the events leading up to his mother's death, except in the briefest possible way. Guy had never been quite old enough before, and certainly children were given only the merest information about the 'events' - but it did seem to be the right time now to talk about the past.

Guy was developing the kind of sensitivity inherited from his mother and his growing maturity meant that he would be well able to play his part in the future of the wider community. Benedict had a feeling that Mystica came from that region, the area of his life that had been extinguished some years ago. He wasn't looking forward to dredging up too many memories, but he needed Guy to understand something of the past. The young were the ones who had to ensure the survival of the future and knowing what to avoid would constitute part of that.

"And this lady," went on Guy, "do you think she might have come from First City? Could she be part of the spy system, checking out where we are, where people are hidden?"

"A bit drastic to nearly drown oneself in order to get hold of information, I'd say! There's something unusual about her, just something I can't quite put into words. I'd be interested to hear what you think."

"So, people went off the rails a bit and the governing lot were too controlling. Is that it?"

"Well, sort of."

"But you said things had happened. What things?"

"There were a series of catastrophes that kicked it all off with Man playing at being God, Man deciding that he can exhaust the earth, Man deciding that he can take by force what is the birthright of humanity, Man deciding that each individual part of him is superior to the rest. A series of wars, famines, freak weather conditions, civil unrest, political tortures, religious hatred all added up to world-wide problems, to chemical changes in the atmosphere, particularly above urban areas with heavy industrialisation, biological changes in Man, fear, jealousy, distrust -   all the negatives you can think of."

"That sounds good!"

"Tyranny took over, of course, as democracy was totally abandoned. People had lost confidence in democracy as a form of leadership, disillusionment had set in with weak governments going round in circles of panic. It was all too easy for an oppressive domination by the few to make people feel secure, until it gradually changed and was recognised as a reign of cruelty. Most people were, by then, too frightened to do anything other than blindly obey the rules, however brutal they were. So, a democratic system needs to be considered again as long as equality and consensus remain firmly in the governing body's equation. It has always seemed the most effective way of remedying injustice, but it lost its way in the midst of global catastrophes that seemed impossible to deal with. Democracy, at its best, is capable of reform whenever necessary and the settling of differences peacefully."

Benedict paused to let that filter through to Guy.

"And then, of course, there was the virus."

Chapter 6   Mystica

Mystica woke after a night scorched with dreams. Philip featured in each of them and his face was so vivid, his voice so clear and his smile so warm that tears cascaded down her cheeks.
Philip and Louis. She knew only too well that this man and his apparent betrayal of the system would mean elimination. Maybe the child would be obliterated too, in case the genes that produced him would be duplicated and he should cause twice the amount of trouble in the future.

She lay there in Juno's small bedroom. Juno was fast asleep, oblivious of the sun which was filtering in through the window, displaying dust motes and favouring the room with a warmth and comfort that Mystica could not feel. The dreams faded the way they do, and Mystica tried frantically to hang on to the vision of somebody that had been with her most of the fitful night. She felt as if she was reaching out to something that was unattainable and disappearing. But as she grew nearer to being properly awake, the vision and memory of Philip became more distant and intangible. She could no longer remember anything of the dream images, and when the last vestiges of dream memory had vanished, she was left with a numbness, an emptiness. She could not think of Philip's name. She couldn't even recall his face, let alone his voice. She had lost him altogether.

Mystica's throat felt sore and she thought back to the previous day when she had coughed up half the ocean. Her head ached and there was a large vacant space where her soul had been. She eased herself from the bed and moved on legs like lead towards the window and looked out. The view was veiled in a kind of camouflage cloaking - the light could find the chinks but the dwelling was almost impossible to see from the outside. There was a system of mirrors which allowed the light and the view to make their way into the room and filter across the furniture, illuminating everything with a sympathetic morning glow.

Mystica felt a deep heaviness in her body as she became aware of a tremendous loss, without being able to grasp its content; she just knew that her life had been dealt the kind of blow that would plunge it into uncertainty and suspicion. She had the feeling that she had found like-minded people somewhere, but where? And a lifetime of First City attitudes had endowed her with caution about those she came in contact with, although her mind could not focus on First City. She knew that she hadn't opened her heart to anyone; she believed in keeping her own counsel, a non-descript profile that gave her the opportunity to fade into any background and become a non-person. But then somebody appeared on the scene and all sense of the hopelessness of humanity disintegrated.

She tried to remember what she had felt - it seemed as if it might have been the greatest happiness she had ever known and yet something went wrong, something happened to change it all, but the more she tried to think back the more the feelings and fragmented images faded into obscurity and disappeared.

She looked at the sea in the distance, beyond the dunes, the shimmering of the waves that bounded onto the shore with their white crests foaming, plunging and dipping on the sand. The glorious sight merely filled her with greater despair and she pulled back and managed to make it back to the bed before she collapsed.

Juno woke immediately and, flinging back the bed covering, she went quickly across the room to where Mystica lay.

"Bloody hell," she said. "God, I mean, well, are you OK?"

Mystica smiled weakly.

"I'm alive," she said. "I'm sorry to have given you so much trouble."

"It's not a problem at all," said Juno. "Finding you was the most exciting thing that has ever happened to me, in fact. I mean, well, life is always so dull round here really."

She grinned and Mystica couldn't help smiling back.

"Well, that's one positive I guess," said Mystica. "I wonder if you could possibly get me some water. My throat is unsure of itself and my legs even more so."

"Yes, of course. Wait here. Probably better that you stay put, well, for the moment anyway. Perhaps until Ben has been."

"Ben?"

"Ben. Benedict really. He's our medical man. Guy's Dad. Guy's my friend. Ben's a really nice bloke. I'll get you some water." Juno sprang up and pressed a button on the bedroom wall. A discreet light was activated and a glass appeared behind a small screen, into which the freshest water was poured, glistening and shining, directly accessed from the shared family spring.

Mystica permitted a wider smile. 'Bloke.' She had a distant, far distant memory of an old man using that word in connection with a friend. He always referred to him as a 'good bloke.' Who was the old man? She had a flash picture that shot across her mind.

"Grandpa", she whispered.

This harking back to an expression from the distant past gave her an element of comfort. She felt that perhaps Juno's openness and the care she had been given the previous evening could only come from people you could trust.

What was this place? What was she doing here? How on earth did she get into the sea? And what had happened before that? Everything in her mind was a jumble with an occasional image rushing briefly to the surface, only to melt away before she could hold it.

"We didn't get introduced last night, did we? My name's Juno. I'm the one who is a nuisance to everybody."

"I can't believe that. I seem to remember someone coming to my rescue and sorting me out very professionally," replied Mystica. "I'm ... God, I can't remember my name!"

"Right, we'd better find one for you. What would you like to be called? Given the opportunity to choose, which we never are."

"I have no idea. "

"We could go down the road of mythical sea creatures like, well, like Amphitrite, Thetis, Galatea, or Aphrodite."

"Not too sure about any of those," Mystica responded with a smile. "How do you know all that?"

"Dad. He's an ancient history freak. Well, a bit of a freak all round really."

Mystica smiled and raised an eyebrow.

"No, he's OK really. Well, it's my job to put him down isn't it? I mean, well, he's my Dad. But you can see why I'm called Juno. She was Queen of the Gods, Jupiter's missus. So, an ancient war-like Roman goddess. That's where I get my fighting spirit from I suppose."

" She also gave her name to the word 'rejuvenate' I believe, and that's what you did with me I guess - you certainly brought me back from somewhere. Hmmm, let's see. Amphitrite's a bit of a moaning Minnie I think," said Mystica, "and although Aphrodite rose out of the sea, I think she was a bit of a handful. I mean she was the goddess of love and beauty. Probably not too appropriate."

"And sexuality as well," said Juno.

Mystica laughed loudly. "I don't think so! Not me."

"Well, there's always Doris," said Juno. "She was the wife of a fish-tailed God called Nereus. She was Amphitrite's mother."

"Sounds like a real old duck," said Mystica. "Not sure I like that name. Maybe Dora is softer, slightly more attractive."

"Yes, Dora! That's great. Greek you know, it means 'God's Gift' and perhaps you are just that, to us I mean. But, well, we must find out who you really are."

Mystica smiled. "That's settled then, Dora it is. For now. And I'm not sure how much of a gift I am to any of you. More of a liability. I just wish everything didn't seem so cloudy and muddled. I can't remember anything. How I came to be in the sea or...or anything."

Juno passed her the glass of water and Mystica smiled her thanks. She took a sip and felt a sharpness in her throat as the water slipped across the parts that had been strained through vomiting the sea water. She felt the dryness disappear and a feeling of relief and drained the glass.

"More?" asked Juno.

"Please," said Mystica. "That was so good. Thank you."

At that moment the door opened tentatively and Marnie poked her head round. Juno refilled the glass and gave it to Mystica while Marnie came forward and sat on Mystica's bed.

"So, how are you this morning? I hope you slept OK."

"By the way Mum, this is Dora."

" Dora? Right."

"Well, just for now..." said Juno. "Dora's had a bit of a memory blip. She needs some time I guess to restore the whole thing."

Marnie didn't make any comment about that and just continued.

"Ben gave you something last night that I think would have knocked anybody out, and he'll be coming by later on to check on you."

"I slept well. Thank you. And thank you for your kindness," Mystica replied.

"We are all concerned about you, and we're only too happy to have been able to help in some small way."

Mystica smiled her gratitude but said nothing.

"Maybe you can tell us a little bit about how you came to be washed up on our beach. Where did you come from? Are you in some sort of trouble? Maybe we can help."

Mystica again said nothing but she shook her head, her face crumpled and her eyes filled with the tears she was trying so hard to keep back. She looked down as she felt the convulsive spasms of her repressed sobs welling up. She tried vainly to control and contain her tears, but they sprang from the depths of her soul and she shook and trembled. Juno looked at her mother in alarm and Marnie motioned for her to leave them alone as she enfolded Mystica in her arms and rocked her gently back and forth as if comforting a small child.

"Let it go," she said gently. "Let it go."

"I feel as if I have a rock buried deep inside my chest, pulling me down. Some awful burden, but I don't know what. I don't know who I am. I thought I knew my name, but every time something rises to the surface of my mind, it gets forced back, like a dream you are trying to recall that disappears so swiftly that you can't remember anything except the way it made you feel. And my mind is filling me with sadness."

Mystica no longer held back. The restraint that she had tried to hang on to was overwhelmed by the substance of her grief and she gave in to an all-encompassing, incomprehensible and crushing sorrow. Marnie just held her tightly. Juno moved silently from the room and went to the kitchen where her father and brother sat, looking alarmed.

"My God," said Torrey. "What on earth? What's wrong? I've never heard anything like it. It sounds like the foundations have fallen out of her life; she's just crumbling."

Joseph said nothing but smiled at Juno and got up to start making breakfast.

"I can do that, Dad," said a very subdued Juno.

"I hope Ben doesn't wait too long before he comes," said her father. "I haven't had much experience of dealing with people who are hysterical or desperate or whatever she is."

"She's not hysterical, Dad," said Juno. "She seems to have lost her memory. Torrey was close I think. Something terrible has happened in her life and she's inconsolable, although she doesn't know what or why. I guess we just have to be patient with her."

"Well, you're right I'm sure. Something awful must have pushed her into that despair. I've never heard noises like that before. It's a ghastly, tragic, primitive sound. Not something I can easily handle, but your mother will sort it out."

Juno looked doubtful. She had every confidence in her mother's ability to mend certain surface wounds, to ease the disappointment of young children, to cope with the day-to-day problems that surfaced from time to time in their small community and to dispense normal everyday common sense whenever necessary. However, this was different, and yet she had seen Marnie instinctively knowing what to do, what to say, and witnessed how she just held

Mystica in her arms. Maybe that's what all mothers can do she thought.

"By the way," said Juno, "since she can't remember her name, we've decided, her and me, that her name is Dora. Just for now. Until her memory comes back. If it comes back. Oh my God, supposing it never comes back!"

Chapter 7   Philip

Philip, Samuel and Henny arrived back in the community after a tortuous and difficult journey. Philip needed persuasion to return and it was only the thought of Louis, his one remaining joy that moved him forward. In all other respects, his life was over.

Edward met them at the secret entrance and pulled Philip towards him, enveloping him in a tight embrace. Edward was trembling and emotional. He had come to love Mystica as the granddaughter he had never had, as a natural successor to everything he had achieved within the community; he had hoped that she and Samuel together would have taken up the reins when he no longer had the strength to lead the groups that were amassing beyond First City, slowly but surely, ready to put some purpose back into the lives of the citizens. Edward looked into Philip's eyes and they reflected some of the sorrow that he felt, but with the additional loss of his perfect life partner.

Edward led Philip inside and took him to the quietness of his private quarters, through a glazed doorway that led in turn to a small courtyard. It was warm and had some sort of artificial sunlight streaming down from a clear roof. Beautiful coloured and succulent green plants were strategically placed to catch the glow and glimmer of the light as it fell. A miniature waterfall cascaded gently down from the roof level, over a rough outcrop and it spread an occasional spectrum of light across the courtyard onto the opposite wall.

"This is my private garden," said Edward. "I bring chosen people here on occasions. Otherwise it is my special place. Somewhere I can escape to if the need arises."

Philip knew that this was the space where Edward had taken Mystica when she needed his warmth, where he had untangled some of her deepest interior knots, settled some of her doubts. He felt a sense of peace here with this extraordinary man, and knew that he could at least make a start to feel human again. He had no choice. A huge wave of guilt flooded across him as he thought of how easily he might have given in to abandoning Louis and his heart quickened with misery.

Edward took him to a seat beside the small pool where the waterfall collected. A dragonfly skimmed across its surface, its two sets of wings, shimmering in the light. It pushed upwards and then swooped down to the water level before vanishing among the plant life on the edge of the pool. Philip watched the creature disappear and thought of Mystica, thought of her small pile of possessions left on the beach. Another dragonfly swept across the surface of the water, taking a mosquito that had been idling in the light. Philip watched the order of things taking place. Some live, some die, some make their decisions wisely, some don't even notice what's happening around them, so intent are they on spoiling life for others. He marvelled at the dragonfly and saw it go back to the water again, avoiding touching the surface, seeking its next victim. Such a beautiful creature with an extraordinarily voracious carnivorous nature seemed incongruous. He wondered if the mapping out of every creature's life is inscribed before birth. Perhaps he was destined never to find enduring happiness. Perhaps the dragonfly was one of nature's winners. As he watched, a small frog that had been resting on an outcrop partially covered by some low hanging branches shot out its tongue and, with superior accuracy and speed, secured the dragonfly swallowing it whole.

Edward smiled.

"All creatures have a pecking order and life is fragile, to be taken and enjoyed for whatever span."

"I just can't believe that Mystica and I found something so special and it has just disintegrated. I feel lost without her. I just don't know how to begin again."

"You will. You've experienced something that most of the people in First City never get to feel. The fact that you have had this wonderful love has allowed you to feel one of the deepest of human emotions, grief and loss. Here, in our small community, we have all come to experience the deeper emotions that once were a normal part of living. We have all lost something now. Mystica had made a great impact on us, in the short time we got to know her. We all loved her."

Philip began to protest, "Nobody could have loved her like I did!"

"That's true, but she had a special place in all our hearts. Your grief is the greatest, but we are all suffering. To me, she was the nearest I had to a grand-daughter. And then, there's Brooks."

"Brooks?"

Brooks was a hugely talented but emotionally damaged man who was the technical overseer of the community. He had a brain that understood engineering problems and solved them instantly. He was obsessed by little things and Mystica was the only person who had noticed his aversion to the colour red; she had quietly and without fuss exchanged the gift of a red yo-yo for a blue one that they had won as prizes in a party game to celebrate Edward's 80th birthday. Mystica had become his true friend; she had discovered that he had a particular talent for painting and drawing and his intricate designs displayed the warmth and colour that remained concealed in his everyday dealings with people.

"You know, Mystica unlocked something in the mind and feelings of Brooks and released an emotion that had been stunted by terror and ill-treatment over several years. He will miss her dreadfully. In fact I am not sure just how to deal with telling him what has happened. But everyone must be told."

"And then there's Henny," said Philip. "She seems to have taken the whole thing on her shoulders, thinks it's all her fault."

"It's certainly true that she leapt to the wrong conclusion and I can imagine how heavy that burden must feel, but can we really fix blame anywhere? You could say that you should never have tried to return for what was simply a toy, an important sentimental object with strong associations, but essentially a toy. Perhaps you should not have stopped to talk to Lucas either, since he was under suspicion and not to be trusted we thought."

Philip nodded. "I have thought about that so much. I don't really attach any blame to Henny. She was doing what she thought was best. The responsibility is entirely mine for what happened."

He thrust his hands up and covered his eyes.

"But Mystica had some responsibility for her own actions as well," said Edward. "She had time to ensure that she had packed everything essential, and the inconsequential things as well, before you left. She had ample time to pack her snow-globe. She should have insisted that the globe had to be left behind. It would have been safe with us. She could have collected it another time. She should never have allowed you to return."

"I'm not sure I gave her a lot of choice," said Philip. "I was so intent on the sentimental side of things; I wanted her to have everything from the beginning just the way it should be. I shouldn't have left her, of course I shouldn't."

"But again, perhaps she should have thought more carefully when Henny caught up with her. Henny is young, inexperienced, may have got it wrong and Mystica had the advantage of maturity and wisdom. Perhaps we might think she ought to have questioned Henny and gone back with her to find out for sure what had happened. Love does funny things to people. Blame cannot be attributed to any one person, but only to circumstance and that is something that you, and Henny, will need to understand."

Chapter 8   Henny

Henny had hidden herself away.

Instead of the outgoing, exuberant, fun-loving individual she had been before, she felt lost, guilty and ashamed. She felt the blame for losing Mystica rested fairly and squarely on her shoulders. Her mother, Ava, who looked after the domestic arrangements for the community, had no idea what to do. She had never seen Henny like this before and whenever she tried to talk to her, Henny pushed her away or walked quickly out of reach.

Henny wasn't eating. For a growing girl with a huge appetite for the good things in life, very much including food, it was almost as if she felt she could expiate her dreadful sin through a penance that involved fading away.

She took no notice of what she looked like, whether she had brushed her hair, what clothes she wore.

She moved away quickly if anybody approached her and tried to talk. She sat for long periods of time huddled in the darkest corner she could find, going over and over the events of the past few days, trying to find a way of erasing the past and starting again.

If she slept, her dreams were full of darkness and misery until one day when she dreamt that everything was fine. Nothing dreadful had happened. Philip and Mystica were still living within the community and she had special care of Louis to herself. She woke with a lightness in her heart, which started to evaporate rapidly as she realised the awful truth. She felt a great lump in her stomach and it felt as if her heart was beating at double its normal speed. She clawed at her brain, frantically trying to hold on to the dream but, as it continued to fade, she cried out; an agonised desolate and convulsive sobbing took over. Ava rushed in, wrapped her arms round Henny and rocked her gently to and fro until the worst of the grief started to ebb and the tears shrank back into the dullness of her being. She felt disabled, crippled in some way, her heart undermined. But she knew that she had very much needed her mother's quiet presence and comfort.

There was a silence, but Henny continued to hold on to her mother tightly. Ava smoothed the hair from Henny's wet face and wiped away the grime of tears. She kissed her gently on her cheek.

"I need some help today," said Ava. "Just stacking and sending back to the units via the individual ports. I'm too busy to do that at the moment without working overtime, so it would be a help. There's nobody else there. No-one to come and ask questions. What do you say?"

Henny said nothing. She just nodded and stood up. Ava and Henny walked out hand in hand.

In the community cleansing section, the machinery whirred quietly and comfortingly. There was a feeling of being enveloped by something familiar and friendly, warm and predictable. This was the element of the community that was Ava's special domain. She watched over every aspect of the cleansing of the unit, with its high speed dirt and infection facilities filtering out all the unwanted particles; articles were cleaned and refreshed, ready to go. Kitchen items went in one machine, upholstery in another, clothing that needed special treatment in several separate machines - depending on whether the article is fragile, filthy, needed a high temperature, a low temperature. At the touch of a button the clothes were robotically sorted, categorised and dealt with.

Ava wore a smart tunic in a delicate shade of blue, which matched a pair of stunning blue eyes. She passed across a tunic for Henny who put it on over her clothes, her own sharp blue eyes far away. Ava placed a set of dirty working overalls on the front end of the belt, together with two bed sheets, a gossamer thin silk dress and four or five shirts. She waved her hand over the wall switch and the machine was activated. Silently, the package of clothing sped through its porthole and disappeared from view.

Henny walked down the room, to the despatch section, past other conveyor belts waiting for their goods. She arrived at an empty belt that silently started moving as she reached it. Through the porthole came a pile of neat, fresh clothing that had been categorised, pressed and dealt with instantly. Henny looked at the labels and automatically placed the cleaned laundry in the delivery chute; she knew that all the separate items, according to how they had been labelled, were sent to the appropriate section: personal goods by name, kitchen items to the kitchen store.

EDWIN, the electronic internal transporter system (its acronym standing for Electronic Delivery With INtelligence), moved silently into action and Henny was grateful for a mindless task that just required manual loading and no brain work.

Chapter 9   Benedict and Guy

"So tell me about the virus? They come and go, don't they?"

"Usually, but this one didn't. It was unlike any virus previously experienced. The symptoms were so diverse - temperature, cough, aches and pains which were normal virus fodder - but also loss of sense of smell and taste, huge spikes of depression, lung scarring and great physical weakness. People felt they were recovering only for the whole thing to emerge again. There was no treatment that appeared to help and no vaccine available to prevent spread of infection."

"Shit!"

"Shit indeed. Epidemiologists, infectious disease specialists, virologists, experts in every imaginable medical specialty worked tirelessly to beat the thing. Life was pretty intolerable for many people, and the virus was no respecter of age, ethnicity, wealth, intelligence - if you were in the wrong place at the wrong time and met someone carrying the virus it attached itself to you, unless you had some personal immunity."

"So some people didn't get it, even though they were in contact with carriers?"

"That's right. It was completely unpredictable. Whole areas had to be shut down; people had to stay in their homes, until a testing of the infection rate suggested that it was safe to come out of isolation."

"And did the virus die out then? I mean, we are talking years ago aren't we?"

"Well, yes sort of. A suitable vaccine was found that was given to just about everyone, but it was made clear that the virus would always be lurking around somewhere, and the long-term effects for some people were devastating, with heart and lung problems for the rest of their lives. Many people were too afraid to go back to any form of social living with friends and family. Many were afraid of the vaccine itself. On the plus side, the lack of travel and so on meant that the earth had some breathing space and time to recover. Those at some sort of government level knew that radical changes needed to happen. The Restoration Plan was eventually put in place by people with a determination to try and restore the balance and, to start with, Edward was one of them.

"And also, did this happen everywhere? I mean throughout the world? It seems a bit extreme."

"My understanding is that the same sort of system collapse happened pretty much in all the so-called civilised countries in the world. The ease of communications everywhere latterly made it impossible for the rot to remain among isolated nations. It spread. The ability to send details of horror and ghastliness within a nano-second to the farthest outposts of our globe has had the effect of telling people too much, too soon and, like Chinese whispers, reality got distorted and truth disappeared. "

"What will happen to First City? Will Edward ever be able to get things back to some stability?"

"I'm sure, but it may not happen in his time. He is very fit, but he's an old man and he must be pretty tired these days. It will need the help of your generation and a return to old-fashioned values that nobody really remembers any more, coupled with a greater insight into how and why these can get distorted and what to do about it when they do - without taking away personal liberty, destroying self-esteem."

"What do you mean?"

"Well," said Ben, "years ago people were put in small single units and locked away as a punishment for behaving immorally, illegally, or outside the government system - sometimes they had killed or raped, sometimes they had defrauded or stolen."

"Was that what they called 'prison'?" asked Guy. "It sounds barbaric whenever I read about it."

"Yes. Don't forget, you live in a very small closed world where the concept of living together makes our people look out for each other. It has become unthinkable for us to do anything to hurt others in our community. And I guess on the very few occasions when anyone does something socially unacceptable, it is dealt with by that individual who sees how much his or her actions have an effect on the rest of us. Usually there is little need for corrective measures; we have become a self-correcting community, but we're all different. Some people have a shorter fuse than others, some are not so aware of the sensitivity of their neighbours, some have feelings of envy, some have to work hard to control greed, some are lazy. Outbursts are not uncommon."

"But nothing too awful ever happens here does it?"

"No, fortunately not. But on those rare occasions when something does get out of kilter it becomes necessary to talk matters through with someone; that is what your mother was so good at. She possessed great wisdom and an extraordinary capacity for seeing goodness in others, even those the rest of us might have had little time for. She had a wonderful ability to help and advise and never made judgements on anyone."

"I wish I'd known her."

"She was my life companion. I was so lucky to have her, even for a limited time. She was very special to everyone she came in contact with. I think you have a similar capacity and your special qualities will be of great value in the years to come. We are at a transition stage. Edward is gathering people together and, when the time is right, those who have been moved to accept that the situation at present is almost as evil and corrupt as the one it replaced will be the ones to help change direction."

"I'd like to be part of it. I'd really like to be able to help. But, surely there will always be people who are potentially evil, those who are greedy and those who have no moral standpoint. What do we do about them?" asked Guy.

Benedict nodded.

"All humanity is potentially corrupt," he replied. "Education, compassion, strength are the ways forward. Fifty years ago prison was an accepted way of dealing with criminals, the perpetrators of evil. They were kept there for a certain length of time and then released with nowhere to go in particular and nothing to stop them repeating their previous offences. Sometimes it was felt that the laws were unacceptable, as they displayed a certain inequality to rich and poor and the rich could afford to pay for the best possible defence teams. The poor had to rely on the less experienced defenders or those with poor track records, when a system of legal aid was ended."

"I don't understand. Legal aid? What was that?"

"I think it was a way of securing the best possible defence, to get advice, mediation or representation in court for those who had no funds available to pay for it. It was a way of offering help, but for many of those who lost their court battle, the next stage was probably prison. The taking away of liberty has to be done with the maximum of support to the individual's self-esteem, the greatest possible help in recovering dignity and assistance in educating that person to ensure a process of rehabilitation. People need to be able to take their place in society and to be considered worthy citizens."

"But why did people break the rules in the first place? Were the rules so terrible?"

"For the most part, the laws they were breaking were for the common good, the rules they were flouting were worthwhile, but these were people who had flaws in their personalities, difficulties in their backgrounds and upbringing which meant that they had no personal yardsticks with which to judge what was good and what was evil. They almost always needed extra help in order to see the importance of some kind of code of behaviour. Society was acquisitive; some of the "have-nots" refused to work in order to obtain what they wanted - they chose, instead, to help themselves the easiest way. When the various social catastrophes occurred, anger and hatred erupted, these old-fashioned values disappeared almost completely and an anarchic society became dominant with little respect for order and stability. Something had to change."

"So, do we assume that people are no longer corrupt or greedy? Are there no longer potential problem individuals who may need to be removed from society for whatever reason?" asked Guy.

"Hard to tell really. We are cocooned here in our idyllic carefully-chosen community. I imagine there will always be people who present huge problems to the rest of society unfortunately."

"We need to reinstitute the laws, the social rules, the protocols for standard human life then," said Guy. "But improve them, teach people, make them aware of their responsibility to the human race rather than assuming they have the right to take everything they personally want."

"A big task," said Ben, nodding," but I think you and your generation in our small communities are being brought up to see that more compact groups work better. Things are easier when everyone knows their neighbours. The world had become a bigger place with people blocking themselves off from their neighbours, shunning their communities because they were too large and unwieldy. It was too difficult to get to know anyone other than in a surface way, so the sense of responsibility dwindled and died. We must bring it back."

Chapter 10   Mystica and the Baxters

Juno, uncharacteristically, had gone to the living area and laid the table for breakfast - with an extra place for Mystica.

She had been out to collect the morning's eggs from the small group of Rhode Island Reds who greeted her noisily and with affection. She loved the hens. Not as much as she loved Mouse, but they did show a certain preference for her, over the rest of the family. They were gentle and inquisitive and would follow her round the patch, clucking until she stooped down to touch their feathers. She would talk to them, ask them their opinion on things and they would, of course, tell her exactly the way everything should be. She loved their warm contented clucking. It all sounded so reasonable and simple.

There were four newly laid eggs this morning and she gathered them into her tunic.

"Can't stay to chat today, women," she said. "There's Doris to feed. No, I mean Dora. God, I wonder what her name is? Will she ever remember? I'll bring her out later. Introduce you."

In Juno's room Marnie waited until Mystica was quite calm and all her weeping had stopped.

"Would you like to stay here for a while, or do you think you can face the rest of the Baxter crowd?"

Mystica felt disorientated, but she felt she needed company and didn't want to be on her own.

"I'll join you if I may," she said. "I am really sorry to have disturbed you all. I can't fathom it out. But it was rather taken out of my hands I think."

"You are most welcome. I'm just glad that Juno found you when she did and had the presence of mind to get part of the ocean out of you. Look, I'll go on and you come to the living area when you're ready. There's no hurry."

Marnie left the room and Mystica sat for a moment, feelings of exhaustion coming over her in waves. Then she shook herself and stood up quickly, which made her feel dizzy and she sank back on the bed.

As Marnie went into the living area, Joseph, Torrey and Juno stopped talking and stared at her.

"Well, please don't do that when Dora comes down!" she said.

"The last thing she needs is to be made to feel the focus of everyone's conversation."

"But, I'm afraid that's rather what she is," excused Joseph, "and she could hardly blame us for wondering about her."

"Mum's right though," said Juno. "We must make her feel comfortable - not like some skewed oddball."

"Juno, you put things so well." Torrey laughed and they all relaxed a little.

Taking it slowly and gently, Mystica washed and dressed and went down to meet the family.

"Come and sit down, Dora." Joseph stood up, smiled at her and indicated his chair. Mystica sat and watched as Juno dished up some light scrambled egg for her, with a glass of freshly squeezed orange juice.

"Orange juice," she exclaimed. "How wonderful, but where do you get the oranges from?"

"We have our farming unit here and supply most of the produce for our small community of neighbours."

"But, oranges?"

"Once you know what a plant needs, we can supply it. We have special sections for citrus and tropical fruit, rather like the old greenhouses of many years ago, but here we don't need to rely on particular weather conditions. Everything is simulated, without the bugs! We learnt how to do this from the Guardians..."

Marnie shot him a warning glance.

"... well, from people we had come across a while ago, who did seem able to produce something along agricultural lines," he finished rather lamely. "I have always had an interest in farming techniques and took it on board here."

"I've not seen sunlight like this before," said Mystica. "It is all so clear and beautiful here. I have come from somewhere grey and dull, somewhere clammily cold and dreary. That's all I know. I don't remember where I lived. I just know that life was a sombre thing, not something to enjoy, no spark of light or colour. I only remember neutral powdery air with an almost constant thin drizzle - the sky appeared only to be different shades of grey. Life was just as grey and colourless; enjoyment was not encouraged. But something happened." She broke off and looked disturbed for a moment.

"I can't remember, but I know my life changed...and now this..." her voice trailed away.

"Ben will be here later," said Marnie, "and you might find him a good person to talk to, as well as being an excellent physician. For the moment try not to push yourself. Things will come back to you in their own good time. Try some of Juno's scrambled egg. I didn't know she could make scrambled egg!"

Juno made a face at her mother. "That just shows how much anyone in this house really knows about me."

"I guess it's interesting to know you can make scrambled eggs when you've never done it before," said Torrey and grinned at her. She threw the wet dishcloth at him. He ducked and it neatly hit the window and sagged down smearing the glass on its way.

"What are you like at cleaning windows?" asked Joseph. Juno knew he was teasing and just went over and gave him a gentle push.

Mystica looked across at Torrey. He was a good-looking boy and she wondered what lay behind his piercing blue eyes. She felt a sudden quickening and, in the depths of her memory, she knew she had seen eyes like his before. She looked at Joseph and Marnie and noticed that their eyes were hazel and dark brown respectively. Juno's eyes were just like her mother's, a dark velvety brown. Unusual to have a son with eyes so very different from theirs. As she looked at him she realised that he didn't really resemble any of them particularly. But he certainly resembled somebody from her jumbled past.

"Are you going to be a farmer like your father, Torrey?" she asked.

"No, no. I hope not. Not my kind of thing at all. I'm more academic really. And more artistic."

Juno hooted with laughter and the dishcloth came flying back in her direction.

"I'm the one who understands the soil and the workings of plant life," she said. "He hasn't a clue."

Marnie put her arm round Torrey's shoulder and gave him a hug. "He is an artist. He's a designer in embryo," she said. "He can visualise things that he's never had the experience of seeing in reality and he can design and construct all sorts of items. Many of the bits and pieces we have here have been designed and made by Torrey."

She pointed to a musical instrument standing upright in the corner of the room; it was a sort of guitar/mandolin hybrid, the body made from wood and strings apparently from some manufactured wire compound.

"But that's beautiful," exclaimed Mystica. "Where did you find the wood?"

"There are forestry areas behind the coastal hills. We use the wood for all sorts of things and I just purloined a section for myself. I had to soak the sides in order to make them pliable for bending. This is maple but mahogany is better. No mahogany round here, so I had to make do."

"And, do you play it?" asked Mystica.

"After a fashion. I'm teaching myself and I like experimenting with the sounds I can make."

"I'd love to hear you play some time."

Torrey blushed and said "Well, I'm not that good, but I can play something for you. Do you want to hear something I wrote myself? It's pretty basic, not very good really, but I'll get better!"

"Oh, yes please! I'd love to hear it."

Marnie passed around some sourdough toast and refilled mugs with coffee as Torrey picked the instrument up, sat on his stool and ran his fingers across the strings, barely touching them it seemed. The sound was unlike anything Mystica had ever heard before. It studded the room with brilliance and appeared to sharpen the morning light. It had an intense sweetness that brought tears to her eyes as Torrey gently caressed the strings, producing such an achingly mellifluous tone. The piece he played was short. He put the guitar back in the corner.

"Well, that's the sort of thing," he said. "I'd like to be able to really play well."

Mystica couldn't speak. She just went to him and put her hand on his arm, looked down and closed her eyes.

"That bad?" he asked, a grin spreading across his face.

Chapter 11   Lucas

Lucas had crawled back into the shadows after approaching Philip. He knew he had to return to Polly and their daughter Phoebe, but he had so little enthusiasm for family life, as he knew it, that he felt a heaviness in his chest. He wondered just how much longer he could keep up some pretence of the smooth workings of a family unit that he loathed.

Polly had been favoured by the High Council and she was a trusted Observer. There were some perks to being her partner. He was, for instance, left to his own devices much of the time. However, he was aware of how careful he had to be. Polly suspected everyone and would not hesitate to denounce him too if she had any inkling of the way his life seemed to be moving. She was fanatical and had earned her wings by watching the movements of characters suspected of being subversive to the regime in some way.

It was Polly who had watched and followed Philip's wife, Jo, as she started to make enquiries into the death of her father. It was Polly who had witnessed how close Jo was getting to the truth and how dangerous that would be to the High Council. It was Polly who watched as a girder swung loose and crashed into Jo at work rendering her brain-dead in a split second. It was Polly who warned the hospital staff that questioning what happened was ill-advised. It was Polly who turned a satisfied eye away from Philip as he floundered in widowhood and experienced the difficulties of being a single parent. So it was Polly, the keen Observer, who missed the stirrings of love between Philip and his neighbour, Mystica. She failed to see a developing scenario, a new forbidden relationship that defied the dictats of the regime, until Philip and Mystica had vanished, taking little Louis with them. She felt she had completed her job, Jo had been crushed. She took her eye off the ball. Unusual for her.

And then, there was Phoebe, who could perhaps have been accepted as a teenage rebel, sullen and unresponsive, if it weren't for the gleam of satisfaction that Lucas noticed every time Polly reported the result of some new horror that had removed someone, quietly and efficiently, from society when it seemed that they didn't toe the line. Phoebe was the physical image of her mother and Lucas could find no smidgen of himself in her looks or her personality. It seemed that there wasn't even the remotest dash of Lucas in Phoebe, but maybe he just chose to believe that. It was easier than seeing any of his own faults replicated. But his greatest fault, he knew, was weakness, a subject for manipulation and Phoebe would never be manipulated. Sometimes, in fact, he wondered if she were really his. But then, Polly would never have conceived a child outside the established unit, so he accepted reluctantly that Phoebe must, indeed, be his daughter.

Perhaps, his one saving grace was his ability to fade into the shadows. He was seen by his wife and daughter as a non-person on the whole, and therefore largely ignored. This did give him the ability to do his own observing, unofficially, and totally unrecognised.

Back in his living unit, he saw that he was alone. The apartment was quiet. He savoured the emptiness, the calm, the wonderful feeling that he could think what he wanted and his face could not betray any of his thoughts. It always seemed to him that, when face to face with either Polly or Phoebe, his mind was open, naked and transparent. He was always careful not to show any emotion, his conversation was bland and inconsequential. It was clear that Polly and Phoebe despised him and he rejoiced in that - it made everything simpler and he could continue a lonely existence while he planned his future. He would have been shut out from all their discussions had they imagined for one moment that what they said held any interest for him. They merely treated him as a nobody. As far as they were concerned, he wasn't there. He saw to all his own needs, made his own meals, slept separately, came and went silently and they hardly noticed he was there at all.

He had cultivated anonymity and this, of course, was his great talent. He had stored away items about local people who had come under suspicion. He did nothing about any of the information, since the lapses were slight and would call for minor reprimands when reported to the High Council, nothing more. But he listened and took note of any mounting transgressions, knowing that offences piling up would be dealt with harshly and sometimes, as in the case of Philip's partner, Jo, there was no come-back, no way to redress the balance. The damage was already done and redress was not possible. The High Council had no place for anyone likely to upset the balance of life. They had neither the time nor the inclination to control those who broke the very proper limits. Getting rid of the problem was the only way forward.

As Lucas looked round the apartment, he noticed Polly had left her notebook on the table. She wasn't usually that careless. Didn't leave things lying about. It seemed natural to open it.

Chapter 12   Mystica

Benedict came to see his patient at midday. The sun was streaming through into the living area and Mystica felt a sense of contentment in the unaccustomed warmth, tinged with an uneasy feeling that something was dreadfully wrong in her life.

"Why don't we go outside into the sunshine?" he said.

"I'm just about to make some fresh coffee for us all," said Marnie. "Would you like some too, Ben?"

"Yes please. That would be nice."

He and Mystica stepped outside. They walked slowly to a wooden bench under an apple tree and sat in its shade. She had never seen an apple tree before and looked at it with astonishment.

"This tree?"she said.

 He looked at her and smiled.

"Apple, and a good variety. How do your legs feel?"

"Strangely wobbly," she said. "But I'm more concerned about my brain. My mind seems to have achieved a blank status and I just cannot remember anything. Not where I came from, not why I was in the water, not even my name! Juno has decided I shall be Dora for the time being. A pretty name, but not mine. However, I shall borrow it for now."

"Right, Dora it shall be - for now. I can see that all is well. You have a good colour and the wobbliness is partly shock and I expect your thrashing about in the water gave your muscles a bit of a going over. They'll get stronger in no time. The loss of memory is probably attributable to trauma of some kind. I would say, in your case, a mixture of whatever happened before you hit the water and the conscious act of having to survive. "

"I just don't know what to do. I can't stay here, wonderful and welcoming though the family has been; I get the feeling I was on my way somewhere - but where? And how do I get back on track?

How do I start to remember? Every time some fleeting thought comes into my mind, I seem to chase it away as I frantically try to grasp it and hold on."

"I think the best thing is to see the next few days as a complete 'brain holiday' " said Benedict. "Stop trying so hard. Your mind needs a bit of time to work through everything that might have happened. It will come back, I am sure, but perhaps in its own good time. For the moment, I know that Joseph would welcome another pair of hands with some small harvesting jobs. I doubt they are in any hurry to see you go. The pace of life here is fairly slow and certainly about as stress-free as it is possible to be. Juno, in particular, will very much welcome the distraction. She is a great girl but she's going through the usual mid-teen years with nothing to really kick back against and this is a deep frustration. You could be a very happy diversion for her and the rest of the family. The trouble is her parents are too nice!"

He laughed and she noticed that his whole face seemed to light up. It was infectious and she began to laugh too.

"My parents were very like them," she said.

"Really? Well you seemed to have remembered something."

"That's true," said Mystica, "so I have. But it is a feeling, deep inside. I just know that my parents and grandparents were the best I could have wished for. I can't remember their faces, or their voices and I miss those memories, but I feel some sort of, I don't know, 'presence' I suppose. Wrong word, but I can't come up with anything better, right now. Unless I am living in wishful thinking territory of course, but the feeling is strong. I know I was much loved by them, before ... before I wasn't allowed to be loved ..."

She broke off in some confusion.

"I imagine there's a lot of remembering to be done," said Benedict. "Some of it may not be happy or welcome, but it will need to come back so that you can go forward. I'll be here to help you to cope with the bits that are difficult as they arise. But we can only cushion you so far and you will find some memories easier than others to manage. In the meantime, I think you just need to rest and recover from your dip in the ocean."

"I know some things are likely to hurt. But I also know I must find out. I can't go through the rest of my life in a kind of pleasant fog that seems to have flashes of clear sky pushing it away every now and then before descending again with great speed. I shall work on it. I have to."

"I know. I imagine I would be the same."

Marnie came out with two steaming mugs of freshly brewed coffee. She set them down on the grass in front of the tree.

"So, what's the verdict, doctor? Will the patient survive?"

"Clean bill of health, really. But I prescribe some Baxter hospitality and a bit of a rest altogether. Well, maybe not altogether I suppose. I have just recruited a farm helper for Joseph. Some easy physical harvesting jobs, if such exist, will give a bit of fresh air and exercise and I am sure you could do with some help somewhere along the line. She's already getting the feel of what can grow hereabouts."

Mystica smiled at them both. "Well, an apple tree!" she said.

"Joseph would be grateful, I know, since neither Torrey nor Juno seem too keen to get out and help with the farming. But we will all benefit from you being here. Torrey already feels he has made a friend with musical sensitivity, I shall certainly welcome some sane adult female company and Juno will just love to have you around. She may pester you a bit, although I have given her strict instructions not to. But very little excitement ever comes this way and she does so love a mystery."

At this, Mystica's foot shot out in front of her, knocking over the mug of coffee.

"Oh, I'm so sorry! But that's it - I'm a mystery," she exclaimed.

"No problem," said Marnie. She picked up the mug and looked at Benedict, her eyebrows slightly raised in query.

"Juno!" she shouted. "Can you please bring another coffee out for Dora please?"

"No, no. Not Dora, it's not Dora. Mystica. It's Mystica."

Benedict and Marnie turned to Mystica.

"That's my name. I'm Mystica."

Chapter 13   Philip, Brooks and Henny

Brooks was in his workshop repairing a small part of the touch-sensitive hub that controlled the wall systems throughout the unit. He had put the system on to its secondary standby, so nothing had closed down. Everything was working as normal, but he was a belt and braces man and every part of the equipment in the unit worked on the basis of back-up and extra back-up, which ensured the smooth running of all operations. Only Edward was aware of how lucky they were to have somebody with Brooks' dedication to his machinery, to the wellbeing of the inhabitants and to the physics of life itself. Brooks kept an eye on everything; each tiny compartment of electronic technology was monitored on a regular systematic basis. It was his life.

The workshop door opened and Philip tentatively stuck his head round. Brooks continued with his task, seemingly unaware of the interruption. Philip walked over to the workbench and stood still, looking at Brooks, who eventually put his work down and faced Philip.

"I don't know what to do, what to say," said Philip. "I think you loved her too, but she's gone. She's just gone."
Brooks turned back to his workbench again and said nothing. He adjusted his glasses to sit closer to the end of his nose and concentrated on the job in hand.

"I needed to come to you," said Philip. "I thought you would be the person who would understand how I was feeling. Edward is wonderful and...and so is everyone really I suppose, but you have a greater depth I think than anybody. I think you understand the core of things."

The only sign that Brooks may have heard what Philip had said was the slightest narrowing of eyes, the merest buckling of lines across his forehead.

There was a long silence and Philip wondered if he had made a mistake. Perhaps he shouldn't have tried to involve Brooks in his own feelings.

"Sorry. I shouldn't interrupt you when you're working. Sorry. I'll go."

He made to walk away. Brooks then turned and looked at Philip. "You've got to move on. What's done is done."

Philip could feel tears starting to spring at the corners of his eyes and he began to shake. Brooks put a hand on Philip's arm.

"There's nothing you can change. We're all part of a big map and her route has taken a different turning."

"But, we've lost her," replied Philip. "She's gone. She's dead."

"Did you find her body then?"

"There were footprints in the sand to the water's edge. Nothing came back. I think she deliberately ended her life. We... "

"But you can't be sure. And why would she do that? Yes, she thought you'd been taken, but that wasn't right, now was it? There could be some other answer. And, anyway, she wasn't made of suicidal stuff."

Philip stared at him in bewilderment. Brooks had come alive to make what was probably the longest speech of his life. He retreated as quickly as he had emerged from his particular shell and turned again to the workbench.

"Now you need to get something to do. I'm busy."

Philip walked to the door and stumbled out into the passageway, straight into Henny. She looked embarrassed to see him, but there was no way of avoiding the meeting.

"Oh God, Philip. Philip, Philip, Philip! I don't know what to say. I'm so sorry for, well, everything I guess."

She started to cry. Philip felt uncomfortable and he wasn't sure what to do.

"Stop a minute, Henny." Philip put his hands out in front of her, palms uppermost. "Please stop."

Henny sniffed and gulped and then set her face straight.

"No, I mean I feel to blame in a way. I mean I should have been more careful what I said to Mystica, but I wasn't thinking straight. I suppose I panicked. But I thought she'd just come back with me and we could sort everything out. I didn't think she'd run into the sea like that. Oh God I'm so sorry! It was all my fault."

She was about to cry again. Philip looked her full in the face and took her hands.

"Henny, look, you weren't to blame in any way. You were doing what you thought was for the best. It didn't meet with quite the reaction you expected, but that wasn't your fault. If blame is to be attached to anyone, it should be to me. How foolish I was to go back, retrace our dangerous steps, all for the sake of a plastic cat in a swirling toy snowstorm. What an idiot. But then Mystica was a grown woman. She was able to make choices and she chose to run. We don't know where she ran to."

Philip could feel his own tears close to the surface and he looked down quickly at the floor.

"But, that's what's so awful. We do. I mean, she so obviously ran into the waves. Those footprints only went one way. To decide to drown yourself..."

Philip looked up at her and she saw his grief-stricken face.

"Oh God, I'm doing it again!" she cried. "I'm sorry. I'm just such a...child, I guess."

Philip put his arms round her and hugged her tightly. He looked on her as a younger sister and felt the need to comfort her.

"Look," he said, thinking of what Brooks had so clearly pointed out, "there was no body, nothing washed up as far as we could tell, so we just don't know for certain what happened. On the face of it, that's what it seems might have happened, but we can't make assumptions. And, as someone said to me a short while ago, what's done is done. Let's just try and repair ourselves in some way. We certainly won't be much use to the community if we sit around and beat ourselves with imaginary sticks."

Henny liked the feeling of being hugged by this grown man, the man for whom she had once felt a schoolgirl crush, but this time there was nothing beyond the need for reassurance and forgiveness. For the first time since she had met him, an age gap had crept in, and Philip suddenly seemed incredibly ancient to her. She was silent for a while and just enjoyed being held, and then she broke off and looked at Philip.

"I'm doing some work on the passageway walls," she said. "Edward asked me to paint some scenes on them. I haven't done anything yet, only some rough sketches, but I will make a start tomorrow. Would you look at my ideas and give me some feedback?"

"Of course I'll have a look. I'd like that."

"I hope you like it but I can take hard criticism, you know. I don't want you just to say it's all great. I mean, it might all be crap."

Philip smiled. Yes, she was still a child.

Chapter 14   Mystica and Benedict

Mystica's head was full of jumbled images. The fact of remembering her name seemed like a giant leap forward, but it also was the possible harbinger of future unhappiness. She realised that each stage of remembering was the signal for potential grief and she felt the heaviness without knowing why.

She fought hard to retain some of the fleeting images that misted her mind; she tried to make sense of what was happening. It was like the edge of a dream after awakening. She felt a sense of loss and a vague feeling of what had gone, but the more she tried to work it out the more it slipped back into the deeper recesses of her mind. She tried frantically to reach it, to make herself remember, but it seemed a monumental task.

"I think I might risk going for a walk. Try and clear my head," she said. "I won't be going in the water," she added.

Benedict thought the fresh air would do her good.

"You've recovered well and you need to build up your strength. Do you want any company?"

"No, no thank you!" said Mystica and then thought how ungrateful it must sound. "Do you mind if I just walk alone a bit? I think I need silence to try and sort my mind out."

"You'll get there. Perhaps I'll come out a bit later. See how you're getting on. Would that be OK?"

"Of course. I'd like that."

"Just keeping an eye on my patient."

Marnie walked with Benedict to the door. Mystica could hear them talking quietly and then the door closed and Marnie returned.

"He thinks you're doing wonderfully well. Once the memory starts to return it can come back in big chunks or small flashes, but it will come back. It's already started and that's exciting!"

Mystica felt only a deep heaviness. No excitement. She knew that when her memory returned she was going to have to face some difficult and possibly heart-breaking fragments of her past.

Mystica walked out into the warm sunshine. She breathed deeply and, in spite of feeling an indefinable burden, she experienced some joy in the scent of the salt air and the sound of the surf breaking on the shore and receding. These were new experiences and she made up her mind to take pleasure in each fresh event and occurrence that was put her way. There had to be some purpose to her finding the light and the colour that had been absent in her world.

She made her way through sea grasses and down a makeshift pathway of pebbles and rocks until she was on the sand. The tide was on the turn and the sand was wet and shimmering with undulations and dotted with tiny shells. The waves danced and glistened in the full sun. The warmth on her face was novel and calming. She felt an unexplained happiness, though it was tinged with the frustration of the forgotten elements of her life and the feeling of being at an extraordinary crossroads. Which way should she go? Which way could she go? What was to happen next, and where and how?

She walked from one end of the beach to the other and sat on a large smooth granite rock, staring out to sea as the tide receded. She tried to commandeer her brain into activating her memory, but found it was hopeless. The more she tried to remember, the less anything came to mind. She continued to sit and let her mind close down. Emptying her head and giving in to nothingness was comforting. A feeling of contentment went hand in hand with giving up the quest for recollection. She closed her eyes and faced the sun, glorying in the soothing reassurance of warmth. She rejoiced in the sunlight coruscating across the tops of the waves and she watched as little torn clouds chased their shadows over the headland. But there was something missing, an emptiness. However, she was at ease and, in her relaxed state, felt herself drifting off to sleep.

"Well, so here you are!" said a voice.

Mystica woke with a start to see Benedict standing looking down at her. She woke and stood up hurriedly.

"Don't rush," said Benedict. "You're fine. Nobody is after you and you're not required to do anything at present other than continue to get better."

"What's the time?" asked Mystica.

"Does it matter?" asked Benedict.

"The tide's gone out. I must have gone to sleep."

"The tide waits for nobody. Just does its own thing twice a day, regular as can be. Come and look at the rock pools. They're fascinating when the tide has washed past them. A microcosm."

Mystica walked down the beach with Benedict to a rocky area of the bay, filled with pools and clothed in shining bladderwrack that swirled around in the clear water. She knelt down and watched the pools brimming over with life.

"That's wonderful," she said. "I can see the whole world here."

"Can you see those little hermit crabs?" said Benedict. "They like to live in the shells of other sea creatures and they get fierce guarding their new-found territory from other crabs. And there, look at those limpets attached to the side of the rocks. They're almost impossible to remove unless you spring a great surprise on them. That's a common periwinkle and see, over there, two blennies. They're funny little fish, almost as strange looking as the sea-slug."

"It all looks so new to me and so beautiful. Life under the water for them is vibrant and pulsating. I am so definitely a land creature I fear. What a wonderful place to live. You must be so happy and relaxed, all of you. It seems like the ideal community."

Benedict was silent for a moment. Mystica looked at him enquiringly. He swallowed hard and a faint sigh escaped from his lips.

"Life is never as perfect as others might imagine it to be. We have our ups and downs. Sometimes an apparently perfect lifestyle is not what it seems. There is no compensation for love that is missing, and emotional baggage can be heavy."

"I'm sorry," said Mystica. "I didn't mean to pry or to upset you."

"No, no. It's nothing. I lost the love of my life some years ago. I have only just started to talk to my son, Guy, about it. Ellie was the best thing that had ever happened to me. We were perfectly partnered from the word go. It does happen sometimes, usually by accident I think. She was removed from our home unit when I was at the Health Sector. I collected Guy from the nursery quarter and when we got home, it was cold and quiet and empty."

"Where was she? I mean, when you say "removed" what do you mean?"

The idea of removal had stirred a memory.

"She was a supremely understanding, loving person who gave everything to others. She listened and helped many people through some stressful times in their lives. Life for all of us was not supposed to contain anything that smacked of compassion and I think she had ignored the gypsy's warning and, in the eyes of the local authority, she had gone too far and was potentially a threat. So she was removed, taken. Guy and I were looked at with suspicion and I took him to where there was a secret safe haven. We stayed there, hidden away for a while and then, with others, made the journey here to start a new community. Guy was my priority then and it's no exaggeration to say that he saved me, kept me going, preserved my sanity and loved me unconditionally through all my moments of despair. I guess young children have an instinct for what is required sometimes and, of course, he had inherited so much of his mother's generous spirit that his instincts were already there, in spite of being a toddler. I have been the luckiest of fathers."

Something moved around in Mystica's mind. The removal of Ellie from Benedict's life was a chord that echoed in the deep recesses of her thought processes. A young man, a baby, someone lost, a safe haven, a cat. Where did the cat fit in? Small silent clicks were going round her brain but she was unsure of what she had lost. It was all a bit of a muddle, but amid the confusion, she just knew there was a feeling of incompleteness in her life, something she wanted so desperately to catch up with, to retrieve.

"It must have been a terrible time for you. I can imagine the joy of your son had an overwhelming impact on you and that he was a great blessing, but the feeling of loss never leaves, even when you can't recall the nature of the loss."

"Do you know, I had that feeling about you the moment I saw you. I thought there was something about you that stemmed from a great sadness, even though you were, and are, unable to express it. The knowledge of that loss will return in time and I hope that, when it does come back, the passage of days and weeks will have cushioned it at least a bit."

"Ben, thank you. Thank you for everything. I just wish there was something I could do to show how grateful I am to have found such good friends, and how lucky I am to have landed on my feet."
"I don't think any of that will be a problem. My feeling is that you will be an asset to our community."

"Well, I don't know what talents I may have that would be of any use whatsoever," said Mystica, "but I'm willing to give anything a go. I am concerned that, otherwise, I shall be a drag and a bit of a burden on everyone in the meantime. I can't afford to let that happen. I've never been dependent before and I like to pay my way, so to speak."

"Well, I'm a pretty good judge of character and I think you have already made a hit with Juno, who needs a bit of guidance other than her mother's, to come to terms with the ghastliness of adolescence. That, in itself, will earn you the Baxters' undying gratitude. It isn't easy being a teenager in our community, a place where everything looks pretty perfect and there is nothing to kick against. You might teach her to kick in the right direction!"

"I'm not sure I can teach anything to anybody. I'm not sure what I can do at all," said Mystica and a look of doubt crossed her face.

"You know, my character judgement has also registered that you have a quick mind, a great compassion. I see you as someone with a true and undiminished imagination and an enormous interest in life."

His words jerked a memory at once and a fleeting picture of an elderly man appeared in her mind. This flash unsteadied her and she toppled over on the edge of the rock pool. Benedict leant over to catch her before she fell in.

"Steady on Mystica. We don't want to lose you in the ocean again," said Benedict.

"What you just said, those words, they were almost the same as words spoken to me by someone before. Oh, I can't recall who, but he was a wonderful man and I remember an overwhelming feeling of wanting him to be right!"

"Well, I am sure he was right. I've had enough experience of good and not so good people to be able to distinguish one from the other. I have met cowards and courageous individuals. I've known defeatists and survivors."

"Yes, I am a survivor, aren't I? And I have a strong feeling that I was helped in some way, when I was in the water. Ridiculous I know, but I felt some pressure and a sort of guiding hand."

"Ah, then I expect you were helped. Maybe by one of our few young dolphins. They have just started to come back and, for some extraordinary reason they seem to like people. They must be crackers when we did them so much harm! They were almost wiped out at one stage, so it's good to see them again. This one made sure that you're a survivor and I know you are destined to be a good and strong part of a community, to help the new regime move forward. Edward was right in the people he picked and I imagine you may have come across him yourself. Is that so?"

"Edward. Of course, Edward, it was Edward! That wonderful old man. He was a great friend of my grandfather. I do remember that. I remember him. Benedict, things are starting to come back."

She stood up and looked around her, marvelling at the rugged beauty of the grassy granite headland behind her, speckled with gorse and sea asters. She was fascinated by the wheeling flight of seabirds, screeching and dipping up to the cliffs and down into the shimmering water. She had seen few birds of any kind in her life, only the ducks, the ducks at the park in First City.

"First City," she cried. "That's where I've come from. First City. And I remember ducks on a pond and a baby, but I can't remember his name. I know it was a boy. Benedict, things are starting to return, but I feel scared."

She felt herself trembling and her balance felt shaky. Benedict put out his hand to steady her.

"That was our area too, First City. Edward was a godsend to me at a time of huge personal loss."

"A wonderful man. I need to get back there I think. There are things I can't really...my memory is still so jumbled, but I think I need to return."

"You're doing fine, but don't rush it. I am sure every detail will come back and then we can begin to sort everything out."

They started walking back up the beach and it was only when they reached the Baxters' living unit that she realised she had kept her arm locked in his all the way back.

Chapter 15   Lucas and Polly

Lucas had taken a furtive look inside the notebook that Polly had left behind while she was out. There were some jottings about various people under suspicion. Nothing too damning as yet, but he could see it building up. Mystica's name was there and Philip's too. They were both crossed out with a note in brackets to say that they were seditious and potentially unlikely to conform correctly to the regime. It also said that they appeared to have formed some sort of alliance and were now both missing, having taken a small child with them. If found, they were to be taken in front of the authorities immediately and treatment was recommended.

Lucas felt sick and then heard the sounds of Polly and Phoebe returning to the unit. He hastily replaced the notebook on the table, in the same position in which he had found it. This was not before he had noticed his own name written down, with no further details. It was obvious that she was just waiting to catch him out, in order to have him removed. He could just imagine the phony sadness she would display to the authorities. Their whole partnership was a sham.

The door swung open and Polly looked at him with suspicion.
"So how long have you been in?" she asked.
"I came through the door five minutes before you. I was just going to make a cup of tea. Can I make one for you?"
Polly shook her head, saw the notebook and swept it up from the table, placing it in her pocket.
"Are you hiding things from me?" said Polly. "I don't trust you and I've told the authorities that, my partner though you may be, we have little in common and I'm not happy about your reports. They're sketchy to say the least. You are supposed to be my assistant on the

Local Observer team. Fat lot of assistance I get. I have to do it all myself."

"I haven't done anything," protested Lucas.

"No, that's just it. You haven't done anything. Thank the Almighty I've got Phoebe. She keeps her eyes open and her ear to the ground. I know you are not pulling your weight. As I said, I don't trust you. Don't for one moment consider defying the authorities."

"I don't know what you mean" said Lucas feebly.

"I'm sure you're holding something back. You know more than you let on. You're not as stupid as you make out. But, I've told you before - deceive me and you deceive the regime."

"That's ridiculous," protested Lucas. "Why should I deceive you?"

"Why indeed? I don't want to discover that you have been turning a blind eye to things you've seen or heard."

"I haven't done anything," he repeated.

"That's my point entirely."

"I told you before, I have no appetite for cruelty," he ventured.

"Cruelty?" exploded Polly. "You stupid man. You're only being cruel to Phoebe and me, your partner, your daughter. You're such a hypocrite. You only abhor cruelty in one direction. Have you ever given any thought about what might happen to us if you don't behave sensibly? The authorities trust me and I think I can say that I have achieved a certain cachet in their eyes for my activities, but what kind of respect would they continue to have for me if you put everything I do at risk? Fool!"

Phoebe had followed in behind her and, ignoring her father, she went to her room.

"That's just ridiculous," said Lucas and he went to the bathroom and locked the door behind him.

Through the thin wall partition he could hear Phoebe talking to a friend on the cell phone.

He heard his name mentioned but couldn't catch what she said. From the tone of her voice, it was derisory and probably insulting.

She had nothing but contempt for him as a father, and as a human being, and never concealed the fact that, to her, he was pitiful.

"For God's sake" he thought, "she is just a child. My child. What is happening?"

He felt beads of sweat breaking out on his forehead and knew that he just couldn't take much more. There was nobody he could talk to, nobody he could unburden himself to. He had, however, in his cautious solitude, discovered that there were people who might be able to help him, people who did buck the system, people who had a regard for human decency and the right to be a person with thoughts and feelings. He ran water into the washbasin and let it continue to run for a full minute while he stared at his ravaged face in the mirror. He looked older than his years and his complexion was as neutral and grey as his surroundings. He felt an overwhelming self-pity and a total disappointment that his life was so depressingly wretched.

The door handle rattled vigorously.

"How long do you intend being in there? I want to use the bathroom," shouted Polly. "Hurry up, Phoebe and I have another meeting to go to."

He didn't answer but just splashed water on his face. He took his time drying his face and hands and then opened the door and walked past Polly without a word. The cold water had refreshed his mind as well as his face, and he made the decision to seek out the hidden community that he knew existed somewhere in First City. He already knew that Philip had returned to the city and was in hiding and he determined to look for him. He had accosted Philip on his way back to look for Mystica's toy cat in a glass dome snowstorm, but Philip was unsure of Lucas's motives and managed to give him the slip. Lucas had an approximate idea of where the community might be, on the outer fringes of the city, and he resolved to make his way there again and wait until he could make contact.

Chapter 16   Lucas and Edward

Lucas sat at the dining table looking at the recent First City News on his tablet. He read the latest details of what changes everybody needed to make to their exercise regime, what new food items were available and what new regulations there were about fraternising with Loners. The long and the short of it was that the authorities suggested that conversation with Loners should be avoided whenever possible, and minimum time allotted to them on a daily basis. Lucas kept his face impassive while he digested this latest regulation. He was certain that, before long, Loners would be expunged from society. They were a nuisance, they made for difficulties, they were unknown quantities and therefore potential threats and, as such, they would be erased.

Lucas thought of Mystica. He had always had a rather soft spot for her and he was well aware of the fact that she and Philip had disappeared together. He felt a twinge of jealousy, rather like a sharp shooting pain that went up his spine. He was sensitive enough to know that the possibility of love could exist, although he knew it had been denied to him, as it was for most citizens. Everybody did as they were told, the line they trod was safe and didn't allow for mistakes to be made. Life was too precious to make waves. Or was it? Lucas felt the misery in his soul which seemed to suggest that an end to life might be preferable than the one he was leading. Or perhaps he could find out how to make changes.

He waited until Polly and Phoebe had left for their meeting. He packed a very small bag of essentials and moved quietly from the unit to the street. The street was deserted and, having made up his mind to move towards the community he knew in his heart existed somewhere on the outer regions of the city, he felt exhilarated and, somehow, safe. As he rounded the corner, however, he was immediately met by Phoebe returning to collect her tablet which she left behind.

"Where are you going?" asked Phoebe.

Lucas was infuriated that he should feel intimidated by his own child, but decided to err on the side of caution. Anything he said would be reported back to Polly and then presumably entered in her notebook to start the list of his misdemeanours.

"I felt claustrophobic and needed to get out walking. I shan't be going far. It looks as if the drizzle is about to set in again," said Lucas with as much nonchalance as he could muster.

"You know you should not be out wandering aimlessly," said Phoebe. "It doesn't look good."

It doesn't look good! Lucas wanted to slap her.

"My mother would want you to stay at home when she's at a meeting. You should do what she says. You'd better go straight home now. Come on."

She tried to make Lucas walk back with her to the apartment. She took hold of him and turned him round to face home, pushing him in the small of his back. Suddenly, a streak of stubbornness flashed into Lucas's soul and he roughly jerked away from the girl.

"I'll do my own thing," said Lucas. "Thank you. You can leave me."

Phoebe was astonished. She let go of him straight away. He had never argued before. With a unique show of determination he turned on his heel and strode out, not really knowing where he was going. Phoebe was speechless and just stared after him. Then she turned and ran back to the apartment.

Lucas made his way through the quiet grey streets, as a thin drizzle started to dampen his clothing. His hair stuck to his face and he pushed it back out of his eyes and started running, keeping close to the colourless high stone walls, windowless and forbidding. He reached a road intersection and searched recklessly for signs of someone he could talk to. He wasn't really sure what or who he was looking for, but he knew this was the part of the city that was quiet and lonely, perhaps considered unsafe by many. He had no personal feelings of insecurity. He had thrown caution to the wind, but he didn't really care. There was a certain desperation about him and he knew he had to break out of the misery of his life. It was no life at all he thought. He felt he would rather be dead than living with the weight of hatred that filtered down to him from both his partner and his daughter.

His footsteps echoed on the damp pavement and he stumbled across the roadway where he found a small alleyway recessed into the wall. Not knowing if this was likely to lead him to friendly faces, he lurched into the passageway and leant against the wall to get his breath back. His hair was slicked back on his head and his cheeks dewed from the rain as he felt his heart thumping in his chest.

He heard a quiet rustling sound and shrank back as a youth came towards him, cautiously. Samuel had hidden his signature scarlet handkerchief - he was hesitant about this unfamiliar man huddling against the safety of the passage wall.

"Are you alright?" he asked tentatively. "Can I help you at all?"

Lucas no longer cared if he were in safe or dangerous hands.

"Please, please yes. I do need help. I need to see somebody who will help me."

"Where have you come from?" asked Samuel.

Lucas pointed vaguely in the direction of his part of First City but he had lost his sense of direction now and was unsure of which way was home.

"I am a friend of Mystica," he said. "I live in her apartment block."

Samuel looked at Lucas quickly and then said, "Who is Mystica?"

"Well, I suppose I might have got it all disastrously wrong, but I thought you might know her and I really don't care what happens to me if I have made the wrong move here. I thought you were someone who might be able to take me in."

Samuel weighed this up for a moment and then, somewhat reluctantly, he said, "I will take you somewhere where people might be able to help, but I cannot promise anything. And I am afraid I cannot let you see where we are going."

He took his scarlet handkerchief from his pocket and bound Lucas's eyes with it. When he was satisfied that Lucas was quite blinded, he led him out of the passageway and along the pavement, skirting the wall carefully and watching all the time to ensure there were no eyes looking at them. He turned, crossed the road and turned back again to the alleyway. Lucas had been within a whisker of arriving at the community's location on his own, and Samuel was concerned that anyone could have got so close. He hoped it was coincidence. He entered through the hidden doorway, guiding Lucas in front of him and stopped just inside to remove Lucas's blindfold. He spoke very quietly into a small discreet microphone by the door which connected with Edward's office. Lucas stumbled a little and then stared around him at the colourful walls, the lightness, the artificial sunshine. Samuel received a message back from Edward via his earpiece and then led Lucas round a series of corridors, passing several rooms with open doors, all of which exuded a radiant light and warmth. He started to feel almost relaxed as he was taken into a small office, with comfortable seating and a beautiful old oak desk.

Edward stood up and gestured to Lucas to sit in a swivel chair with rainbow cushions.

"My name is Lucas," said Lucas tentatively.

"Yes, I know who you are," said Edward. "But why are you here?"

"I don't know," said Lucas. "I just had to get away. I thought if I found your community you might help."

"You need to know that everybody who becomes part of our community has something, some talent, some gift, they can offer us. And what would you offer? What are your special talents?"

"I...I have none. I'm just a pen-pusher. I can't really do anything."

"I see. Tell me now, your wife, your life partner, Polly isn't it?"

Lucas nodded, unsure as to how Edward could possibly know. Edward noticed the puzzled look on Lucas's face and smiled.

"We know many things, things that don't seem to be known by most people. You also have a daughter, Phoebe, I believe?"

Lucas nodded miserably.

"I have nothing in common with either of them. There is no part of me that seems to have copied itself in Phoebe. I sometimes wonder if she is really my daughter at all. The only advantage I have is that they think I'm pretty worthless. And I guess I probably am. I don't think I can stand being with them any more."

Edward touched a panel in the wall and it slid open to reveal a small tray with two steaming cups of strong coffee. He passed one across the desk to Lucas and smiled at him.

"Well, now, what is happening at home? What sort of thing is Polly up to? Who is she watching? Does Phoebe help her in her activities?"

"I don't really know what Polly is doing but, yes, Phoebe is her right hand girl I suppose. I don't get to hear anything. They go to meetings and they have their own whispered conversations at home and they write in their notebooks, but they tell me nothing."

"Do you have any idea who they may be observing, who is on their hit-list, shall we say?"

"I really don't know much about any of their movements, I'm afraid. I'm always left out of any discussions and if I happen upon them when they are talking about anything they immediately clam up. I really can't tell you much. I've always been too worried about the consequences of delving too deeply into Polly's activities," said Lucas.

"So you really can't help us a great deal, can you?" said Edward gently, although the words themselves sounded rather harsh. "You are not, perhaps, the strongest of individuals, Lucas."

Lucas was again surprised that Edward knew his name.

"I suppose I have been weak. It sounds stupid but I have always been frightened of my wife and daughter."

"Your daughter? But your daughter is just a child Lucas. Isn't that right? Just a child?"

"Yes I suppose so. But she's fourteen and some girls of that age are very wilful, you know. I don't really know how I can help you. I can only list some of the names I saw in Polly's notebook, but they don't mean anything to me, except...well, except my own name was listed, so I imagine Polly has it in mind to deliver me to the authorities.

89

I'm pretty worthless though, as far as they're concerned. I don't do anything to make things difficult for them really. I haven't questioned anything they do."

"Nobody's worthless, Lucas. Well now, "said Edward, "what about these meetings that Polly attends? Who goes to them? What is discussed? Hasn't Polly ever come back and mentioned, even briefly, what the meetings have been about?"

"No, never," replied Lucas miserably. "I don't think I can tell you anything that would be useful at all."

Edward sighed. He didn't quite know what to make of Lucas, but realised that he could be a fence sitter. He could, in fact, turn out, inadvertently, to be far more dangerous to their community if he were not given some sense of worth, a purpose.

"Lucas," he said, "on the contrary, you could, indeed, be a very valuable member of our community."

He smiled at Lucas encouragingly and Lucas felt a small chink of light appearing in his gloomy existence.

"Your huge contribution, however, needs to be made from the outside, from your own surroundings. I need you to return to your home, to patch things up with Polly as best you can and, for now, to do nothing that could antagonise her or give her the least reason to be suspicious of your functions in helping our community. When you feel that she is less guarded, that is the time when you could carefully find out what and who is open to official scrutiny. Your apparent failings in the eyes of Polly and Phoebe might well stand you in good stead. When Polly and Phoebe disregard you, when they pay no attention to you, then their eyes will be closed. You will be a thousand times more useful helping this community and the greater community in general if you could do your own observing and report back. In that way, people in jeopardy could be helped and brought into the potential new regime."

"Yes, I suppose so," said Lucas, "but I can't bear the thought of staying with them any longer than is really necessary."

"And you won't. We will pull you in when the time is right, but we need your help now. Do you think you could manage to do what I ask? It is the best possible way in which you can help us and will benefit everyone, including you - a huge support to the foundation of the new regime. Your future would then be a happy and secure one, but we do still have a long way to go."

"Yes, then I will. Of course. I feel more positive about it all already."

"Good," said Edward and he passed his hand over a portion of the wall. A faint blue light appeared and the door opened silently. Samuel came in.

"Samuel, please escort Lucas back to the street and set him on his way. Make sure he knows the way to a meeting place when it is time for him to return. He may need to be taken a little distance to make sure he is on the right track."

Edward stood up, a broad smile lit up his whole face, and he held out his hands to Lucas. Lucas took them and rejoiced in their warmth and in the assurance that Edward's eyes appeared to promise. He felt calmer and more in control than at any time in the past few years.

Samuel blindfolded him again, after reassuring him that this would not always be necessary, and escorted him back to the dull grey pavements of First City.

"How will I know where to come, when I have something to report?"

"Just come to the place where I found you. Don't worry. I'll find you again."

Lucas made his way back to the empty apartment. Fortunately Polly and Phoebe had yet to return from the meeting and there was a little time to settle himself and decide what possible reason they would need to be told for his walking away from the apartment. He again felt fragile and vulnerable, cold and shivery, and he felt his hands shake when Polly and Phoebe came through the door. There was a silent and frosty atmosphere. However, there were no questions. They chose to ignore him and go to bed.

Sleep was unlikely to be a good companion for him, so Lucas sat up in a chair and tried to direct his thoughts to consider the way forward. At the end of the long, hard, uncomfortable night, he determined to try and keep a very low profile, hoping that his earlier outburst would be forgotten. He got up stiffly and went to the kitchen. A cup of tea seemed to be a good start and he made one for himself and one for Polly and took it in to her.

Before Polly was properly awake he put the cup down, sat on the edge of the bed, and said "Look, I really want to apologise for my behaviour over the last few days in particular. I haven't been sleeping well, but that's no excuse. You have been quite right. I haven't really pulled my weight and I will do better. I have been thinking about it during the night and I am resolved to work harder as your assistant and to be sure that I come up with results that will enhance your position in particular."

She looked at him suspiciously for a moment. Fortunately, she didn't ask him where he had been when Phoebe had met him out in the roadway.

"After all," he said quickly, "whatever you do reflects back on me, so we all win."

He shuffled out - a habit of a lifetime - before she could reply and returned to the kitchen to lay the breakfast table and start the day. This was Lucas, always trying to be inconspicuous. It was one of the things that annoyed her most about him. She didn't always get things exactly right with the authorities, however conscientious she was, and she had made minor mistakes. She now realised that this was her penance. Lucas was the heavy stone that would be forever round her neck, unless he did something so outrageous that the authorities removed him.

Maybe this was something she, or Phoebe, could engineer.

Chapter 17   Philip, Henny and Evelyn

Philip spent some time looking at Henny's work. He was hugely impressed. The mural was a splash of weird and wonderful animals and birds, not one recognisable genus, but the work of a wonderfully fertile imagination. The crimson and violet plumage of fantastic birds of paradise burst through the low hanging branches of trees that shone and glittered with leaves of silver and gold. In the distance a well-fed family of tigers lazily watched a herd of ice-white unicorns, who galloped past with multi-coloured manes flowing in the light breeze across a wide space that dripped with exotic flowers.

"Henny, this is stunning. Your use of colour is incredible. Nobody in First City has any idea that half these colours even exist. How do you know about colour? And these extraordinary creatures? Where did you learn?"

Henny shrugged, a broad smile spreading across her face. She touched her head.

"It's just all in here, "she said.

"This sort of thing is instinctive," said Philip. "You haven't put a foot wrong."

Henny was thrilled that her work made a good impression on Philip. She felt she wanted to please and impress him more than anything in the world. She then pointed to something that Philip had failed to notice. Down in the lower right hand corner, half hidden among the bushes, was a small ginger cat.

"Tiger!"

Philip drew a sharp breath and put his hand across his mouth.

"Is that alright?" Henny looked anxiously at Philip.

"Oh no," said Henny. "God, I'm so sorry! Have I made the most awful mistake...again?"

Philip couldn't speak for a moment. His head spun and his mind whirled round with thoughts of Mystica and the despair he felt at her loss. Tears pricked at his eyes and he turned away.

"Why do I always get things wrong?" said Henny. "Will I never learn? I thought I was doing the right thing. Something to remember her by. Her best friend. Tiger."

Her voice trailed off and she looked devastated.

There was an awkward silence and then Philip turned back and looked at her.

"Henny, Henny, Henny!" he said. "It's alright. You haven't done anything wrong. It was a lovely idea. I'm still a bit raw about the whole business of stupidly trying to go back to collect her Tiger, but I suppose we must never forget the mistakes we make in life or we'll just go on making them. I miss her. I'll always miss her. But, maybe coming back every now and then to look at your mural will bring her back to me a little bit."

Henny looked relieved.

"And we all have to move on, don't we?" she said.

Philip didn't answer for a moment. He knew that her apparent insensitivity was more to do with her innocence, her naive gaucheness, than a lack of tact. She would learn, and her inclusion of the little marmalade cat was meant as a kindness, a token, a consideration of Philip's lasting love for Mystica. He changed the subject.

"Those birds of paradise are superb and I love the unicorns, although I think I would have preferred their manes to be less colourful. They are exotic, mythical creatures and quite striking enough already. The colourful manes make them just a little bizarre. I think, in their case, it's a matter of 'less is more' if you know what I mean."

"Oh yes, you're right. I do know what you mean. They look a bit like those old-fashioned plastic toys in the nursery sector otherwise, don't they? Not quite real? Well, they're not really real anyway, but coloured manes are a bit stupid aren't they?"

Philip smiled thinly. What a child she was, but a child with a considerable talent.

Henny was pleased.

"I said I'd go and help in the nursery. I'm glad you like the mural. I might bring Louis to see it later. Would that be OK? I mean, can I bring Louis and show him? He might remember the cat, mightn't he?"

Philip nodded.

"Yes, sure. I'll be along in a minute."

Henny moved off to the nursery quarter to see Louis and help out with the babies and toddlers.

Philip stayed, staring at the mural and focussing specifically on the little ginger striped cat in the bottom right hand corner. His life had taken on a new meaning with Mystica and he was devastated at her loss, and at his apparent responsibility for this. What piece of stupidity had he indulged in?

That ginger cat. Why was it so special? Tiger had been an important symbol of some kind to both him and Mystica and, like all important symbols, the cat became something that couldn't be overlooked, forsworn or ignored. So, Tiger became the object of their downfall. But maybe Tiger could become an important symbol for Louis also. Philip wondered if Louis would remember Mystica. Their time together, however great the apparent bond that was forged between them, had been all too short.

Philip made his way down to the nursery quarter. The ginger cat in the glass dome snowstorm was in his pocket and he felt the warm smooth ball of glass. It provided some sort of strange comfort, a link to a life that was no more, a link to a fragile love. Perhaps he hadn't deserved that small speck of happiness.

He saw Evelyn talking to Henny, her hand resting on Henny's arm in a warm loving gesture. Evelyn knew what it was to lose someone. Her daughter, Jo, had been Philip's partner. Jo had been too curious about the disappearance of her father, the rules had not been followed and there were too many things that the High Council had needed to keep to themselves. Jo's 'accident' was not a great surprise in the general order of things and there was no way that it could be questioned. So Evelyn had lost the two members of her family. When her partner disappeared she had found her way to the safety of

Edward's community. Jo, as she thought, was safe with Philip, whereas she would always be watched and could be in danger. And then Jo was taken as well. Edward had been delighted to welcome her and asked her to take over the running of the nursery. She loved children and, as Louis's grandmother of course, she had a soft spot for him in particular. She was greatly saddened to think of the loss of Mystica, who was important in Louis's life, as well as Philip's and she, herself, had come to look upon Mystica with great affection.

He went up to Evelyn and she, without a word, took him in her arms and held him tightly. Henny joined in a three-way hug and then sidled off to see to the babies. Sometimes, the girl had moments of perception and she could see that this was to be a private time for Philip with Evelyn. Evelyn, with sorrows of her own, had a great understanding about the need for compassion with others.

"All I sense seems to be a kind of numbness, if it's possible to 'feel' numbness," said Philip. "Evelyn, what shall I do, what can I do? Where do I go from here? I told Edward that I feel lost without Mystica and I just don't know how to begin again."

"Philip, give yourself a bit of space. You have a son and he needs you more than anyone right now. And you, you need him. Take some time out to be with him, talk to him, play with him."

"I don't know if I can play. How can I feel any sort of joy or happiness? How can I stop myself from transmitting my grief to Louis?"

"It will be fine. You just need to connect. Louis will do the rest. Trust me."

She gently turned Philip around and there, sitting on the floor, staring up at him with big round trusting eyes, was Louis. Philip scooped him up and hugged him, nuzzling his face into Louis's tummy. Louis squealed with laughter and suddenly, for Philip, there was a split second of fierce joy. Joy for what he already had, and joy for maybe some happiness to come. And then he felt a great sadness for Evelyn who had, in the midst of her unhappiness over Jo, showed him great kindness. He felt that he had been tactless in the extreme and he realised that lack of diplomacy didn't only belong to the young.

Chapter 18   Lizzie

Philip spent a good hour in the nursery, learning more about Louis than he thought possible. Henny was helping Evelyn to tidy up and clean all the surfaces ready for the next day. Philip sat on the floor, with Louis tucked between his legs and they looked through a book together. Philip pointed to the pictures and said the words out loud. Louis was on the verge of real words and "Da" was his first recognisable one, which he said while jabbing a little finger into Philip's tummy, and pointing to the picture of a man in the book. Philip was captivated.

"Louis, Louis, Louis, you are my best boy, my best ever love!"

As they chatted and played, Philip became aware of someone watching them, sitting on a toddler chair in the far corner. He looked up and saw a girl in her early twenties, and he was surprised that he hadn't seen her before. She gave an apologetic smile.

"Please don't let me stop you. It's lovely for him to have his father read to him."

"We're off now," shouted Henny from the doorway. "All finished for the day. Evelyn says she needs a gin and tonic and I want a long soak in a warm bath. It's these lovely sticky children, you know!"

Evelyn smiled across at Philip and saw immediately that he had just the right person to talk to.

"These children are surrounded by women all day and a man's voice during the "nursery day" is unusual and welcome."

She and Henny slipped out and shut the door quietly behind them.

"This young man is my reason for living," said Philip. "He keeps me sane I think! This is Louis and I'm Philip."

"I met Louis earlier today. He's just lovely and I think we might become good friends. My name is Lizzie and I arrived here a few days ago."

"You must have arrived when I was out, looking for..." Philip's voice broke.

"I'm sorry. I just lost the other incredibly important person in my life and it's difficult to think about her."

Philip then suddenly launched into the events of the previous days. He told this stranger about the extraordinary love that had been given to him by Mystica, their escape to Edward's community with Louis, their plans for a perfect life together, their travel out from the safe area, and finally the ridiculous determination of his to return to that safety in order to fetch the tiger in the glass dome that meant so much to Mystica. Lizzie was silent and listened as he told of his meeting with Lucas, with Henny's mistaken interpretation of the meeting, the loss of Mystica. She didn't tell him that she had already heard about his return to the community, about how he and Mystica had first arrived with baby Louis and about his incredible grief on the loss of this beautiful love he had discovered. She knew all about love and loss and she also knew how important the sharing of sadness was to Philip.

Philip came to a halt and looked at Lizzie.

"I'm so sorry. I'm sorry, I seem to have blurted so much out without thinking. I...I'm sorry."

Lizzie smiled.

"Please don't be sorry. I'm glad you were able to talk about it, and maybe it's easier to speak to a complete stranger who you feel has no background knowledge that would provoke any judgement or criticism. Sometimes one's instincts come into play and it's possible that you may have intuitively felt that I had some similar life experiences."

"I guess so. I haven't spoken to anyone properly, except for Edward, although I am aware that the community knows about what happened a few days ago."

"Edward. That man is incredible! He seems to know the right things to do and say, and has a way of pouring some invisible, intangible healing balm over wounded souls. I know he has helped me to come to terms with my sorrow."

"What happened?"

Philip looked closely at Lizzie and their eyes radiated a mutual trust. But he realised he was prying and she might not want what looked like curiosity. She put a hand out towards him and gently touched his arm.

"It's alright," she said. "Like you, I haven't really talked to anyone except Edward. And I know, when I think rationally, that this is a step towards healing. You have confirmed that by opening up to me, and I can see that you have taken that first step towards recovery. I want that for me."

She noticed Louis's eyes beginning to droop and she lifted the boy gently into her lap. It seemed the most natural thing in the world to Philip that she should do this.

"Please tell me," he said. "You are right. Talking to you here has helped me. I don't feel so lost, the pain doesn't feel quite so sharp, that hump on my back doesn't seem so heavy."

Lizzie took a deep breath.

"I was one of the lucky ones; by sheer coincidence I was partnered by Will, the most wonderful man who I fell in love with. Luckily we had so many good things in common and I knew instinctively that he loved me too. We almost felt as if we shouldn't make it apparent, in case the High Council felt they'd made a mistake! But the more we were together, the more we felt it was appalling that others were not able to have the same wonderful shared tenderness and adoration that we had. Will felt it more than I did. I was content to just be enormously grateful for what we had, but he was angered by the regime. I felt great happiness being in his company and had no need for anything outside that. Will felt an increasing bitterness and we argued about it. I was frightened. I'd seen other people challenging the regime. I'd seen what happened to them."

Philip nodded. His experience with Jo being removed from society when she made too many indiscreet enquiries was always in his mind, and he had developed a great affection for her, even though they hadn't shared the love that Lizzie and Will had experienced. After all, Louis was a product of their partnering.

"I know about that only too well," he said.

Lizzie continued "He thought he could change things, make the system less harsh. He met a woman called Polly who, with her daughter Phoebe, persuaded Will that he could trust them to help him."

Oh God, thought Philip. Polly and Phoebe - a poisonous combination.

"I didn't want to have anything to do with them and we had the fiercest argument I can ever remember. I said some pretty awful things that I regretted as soon as they were out of my mouth. Phoebe made herself rather too accessible to Will and he took refuge in her young teenage arms. He didn't take away her virginity - that had long since been discarded I think - and promised me that there had been nothing more than some mutual "groping" as he put it. I was sickened and it drove us further apart. How do you ever get over that?"

Philip thought back to the time when he had been in a vulnerable position and Henny, young Henny, had been flirtatious to a degree where he had almost taken her to bed. He wasn't sure, even now, if she would have been accepting or horrified, and was relieved to think that he hadn't had the opportunity to find out.

"Something a bit similar happened to me when Mystica and I had a bit of a falling out and I was tempted by the flattering flirtation of someone else. Fortunately, I didn't do anything about it, but it would have been only too easy, had I been in the position that Will was in. Men are a bit more susceptible to that sort of thing. And I would have felt awful I guess if I had given in."

"I can see that. He did give in though, to an extent, but he was also appalled at what he had done and he found it hard to get over his feelings of guilt. Apart from betraying me, he was disgusted at his flagrant "use", as he put it, of an underage girl."

"I knew the family," said Philip. "Phoebe was the most cunning, devious, calculating young teenager I have ever met, and her mother would have encouraged it. She was the Local Observer in our area, and I think used sex as a weapon, for blackmail or anything else she felt would advance her in the eyes of the regime, and obviously training her daughter along the same path. A thoroughly nasty piece of work."

"Will and I had come to terms with the fact that this was a blip in our relationship and had to be thrown to one side. We had too much that was good in our lives, when so many people had nothing but misery. I swallowed my pride, he swallowed his shame, and we got back on some sort of even keel. But of course, time spent with Phoebe and Polly had been recorded and, just as we felt comfortable with each other again, Will was taken for 'treatment'. We were both at home when they came for him. They said he was needed at the High Council to help with some enquiries. Polly had accused him of abusing Phoebe and, of course, she was a well-respected person. She reported that he had almost raped her daughter and her word was certainly accepted over anything that Will could say. Will felt that he probably had abused Phoebe in a way, in spite of the fact that he was given every encouragement by Polly. He implored me not to make a fuss, so for his sake I kept silent and sat watching while he was taken away. The hardest thing I have ever done. I will never forget it."

"And then Edward came on the scene?"

"Yes and very quickly. Edward and Samuel had been hovering in the background, though I have no idea how they knew about Will and me. They did say there was no time to lose, as I was certain to be taken within a matter of hours."

"They also have their own network of observers," said Philip.

"They did some investigating and discovered that Will had been involved in an 'accident'."

Philip cringed, thinking back to when he heard about Jo.

"Samuel was detailed to find me and to encourage me to seek shelter and refuge with them and not to ask any questions from the regime. I packed a few essentials, not enough to look suspicious, and I arrived here on the day that you and Mystica had started your journey out of First City."

"Well, we do have something in common and I am glad you told me. I feel so sad for you, but it's comforting to be able to share in our common grief. You will recover here, as will I. It will all take time, but I am happy to have a friend with whom I can share things that nobody else really knows about or can feel. There are many wounded people here, all with their own stories and backgrounds, all with the need to escape, but some are here purely because of a determination to put right a few thousand wrongs. I feel a special affinity with you, though. I hope that's not too forward!"

Lizzie smiled. She had already found a certain solace and support in helping with the nursery children. Nobody asked any questions and she could spend some time healing herself and in preparation for the future. She found Louis captivating and Evelyn encouraged the warmth that was apparent between the rather sad little baby and the desperately unhappy Lizzie.

"Not forward at all. But I do have another hurdle to jump. My baby will be born in about 5 months' time."

Chapter 19   Mystica, Benedict and Guy

Benedict and Mystica reached the Baxters' unit and she removed her arm from his apologetically.

"I'm so sorry!" she said. "But thank you for making sure I didn't pass out or trip up or anything else remotely connected with a near-drowning!"

"Don't apologise. It was good to have someone, other than one's young son, clinging on. Not that he has done that for a very long time, so it was about time I had someone relying on me to keep them upright!"

They laughed and she turned to go.

"Actually, Guy was asking if he could meet you and I said it was all a bit soon this morning. I needed to see how you were first. You seem to be pretty well one hundred per cent, at least good enough to perhaps spread your acquaintanceship a little. If you could bear to make a new young friend, how about starting with him?"

"I'd love to meet him."

"I'm not a brilliant cook, but I'm marginally better than Guy, so perhaps you could take a chance on eating something prepared in the Eastman household."

"I'm sure you are better than you think and I'd be delighted to try out your cooking."

"What about dinner tomorrow evening?"

"That sounds like a great idea. My diary is pretty empty at the moment, and I'd be out of Marnie's hair for a bit."

"Come earlyish and then you can peel the potatoes."

She looked at him quizzically and smiled. He threw back his head and laughed heartily.

"We may not even have potatoes," he said, "but come early to chat."

She grinned at him and went into the Baxters' unit.

Marnie had seen her coming and gave her a hug.

"How do you feel?" she asked.

"Surprisingly good," said Mystica. "I'm not sure that I should, and there are some big pieces of my personal jigsaw still missing. I think they are the saddest bits that my brain is keeping at bay, but things are gradually returning. What a nice man Benedict is. Having a bit of time to talk to him brought back one or two of the jigsaw's edge pieces."

"He's lovely, isn't he? And his son, Guy, is a joy. I think Guy is one of the few people Juno has any time for."

"I've been invited to meet Guy tomorrow. In fact I've been invited to dinner tomorrow evening, to sample Ben's cooking ability."

Marnie laughed.

"It's basic fare, but wholesome and OK. He's quite a good cook - perhaps not the best chef in the world but I think your company is more what's on the menu for him!"

Mystica was about to protest but Marnie broke in.

"Benedict Eastman needs friends as much as anyone and he has discovered in you someone he can talk to, someone who will understand what it is to lose somebody, or something precious. Perhaps you both need that kind of friendship."

The following day Mystica felt shaky with nerves. How stupid, she thought. I have been invited to have dinner with someone and to meet his son. I am acting as though there is something more to all this. Ridiculous! At the same time she took care over her hair, which she brushed until it shone, using Juno's best bristle brush which had been lent to her for the occasion. Juno was as excited as Mystica and couldn't stop talking about it, until Torrey told her in no uncertain terms to shut up.

"I am sick and tired of hearing about Mystica's 'dinner date'," he said. "The girl's just going to have some food and meet Dr Ben's son. That's all. Stop turning it into the romance of the decade, will you?"

Mystica heard 'the girl' and giggled inwardly. That's pretty how she felt, in spite of her 39 years. Well, she remembered that she was 39 - another small piece of the puzzle.

Juno took Mystica to the Eastmans' unit.
"What do I do now?"she asked. "I don't see a door or a bell or knocker or anything."
"Just wait," said Juno. "You'll see." She gave Mystica a hug and then skipped off back home.
A door slid open noiselessly. There, waiting for her, was Benedict.
"How did you know I was here?" she asked.
"The door told me!"
"Pardon?"
"The door is programmed to open when friends arrive. I just keyed in one or two things - nothing worrying I assure you, just your name, approximate height and the colour of your eyes. The door has a sensor which operates automatically to the programmed information it has received. I can make it refuse to open as well!"

He laughed at the slight look of alarm on her face.
"Come on in."
He led the way into the large, light and airy living area. Sunshine of some kind, unreal and yet perfect, hit the walls and splayed across the ceiling, the light moving almost imperceptively through the space. There was an indoor fountain, playing into a small pool surrounded by lilies, by the side of which were a round table and three elegant chairs, with a bottle of chilled wine and three glasses. Mystica started at the sight of the pool, the plant life, the so natural-seeming artificial light and a memory fleetingly returned. It had Edward in it. Edward, that wonderful old man. She felt she could recall his face and a warmth spread through her body at this perfect recollection.

Guy had been sitting on a low wall on the edge of the pool letting the water play through is fingers. He immediately got up and came over to Mystica.

"Hi, I'm Guy. I've been really looking forward to meeting you."

"Look," said Benedict, "I've got some food to incinerate so I'll leave you two together. Guy will take care of things and pour a glass of that wine. I won't be long, but he's quite tame so you should be OK."

Guy made a face at him and then grinned as Ben disappeared into the culinary section of the unit. Mystica smiled.

"I would say I've heard such a lot about you, but I don't suppose any of us have yet! Hope you're feeling better and that everything you want to remember comes flooding back."

"Guy, thank you. I've been looking forward to meeting you too. I'm feeling much stronger and things are starting to come back to my mind, but thankfully fairly slowly."

"I don't know, but I guess your brain needs time to process each thing that returns, so it has to go slowly."

"Probably, although it is a strange feeling, not really knowing quite who I am!"

"I'm only partly sure of who I am. My mother died when I was a baby so I never got to know her. There's always going to be a part of me that feels missing."

"I'm so sorry. I was lucky to have both my parents for a while. At least I think so."

"Well, my Dad is great of course, and he fills in as many gaps as he can, so I suppose I know a lot about my Mum but I just wish I had had a little time to really know her. I remember almost nothing, except...and this is funny...I sometimes think I can feel her near and smell some sort of scent. Odd really."

"I think that's wonderful. It is a kind of remembering, a kind of inner knowing from a relationship and bond that was very strong. You'll always have that, I'm sure, and it will provide comfort."

"It does, it already does."

There was a small silence between them and then Mystica reached out and touched his arm gently. Guy smiled.

"Do you remember absolutely nothing about where you came from? Nothing about the past at all? You must have come from another beach somewhere to have been thrown up on our patch. Perhaps you were part of another small community like ours, near the sea."

"No, it's funny but I know I came from First City. I recall some travelling and somehow ended up on the beach, don't quite know how and why. That's part of the jigsaw that I can't fill in yet. But, I have the recollection of another small community and all this, this room..."

She spread her arms out wide.

"...this room has allowed another memory to kick in."

"That's really good! Can I ask what?"

"It's the memory of a similar space in this small community I stayed in and a wonderful person called Edward. He had a small garden with a pool and a fountain, like this. It was the most astonishing place. So breathtakingly peaceful."

"Edward! Dad talked about him to me. And about the Restoration Plan, after some event or catastrophe. You must have known about all this as well."

Mystica nodded. She knew, for the most part, about the High Council, the Restoration Plan, the Local Observers, the horrors that happened and she was starting to remember her family. Her grandfather was a good friend of Edward's. It was her grandfather who told her about the hopes for the future after the Green Declaration.

"Yes, I guess I did. Some memories are better hidden and buried I expect."

"But we need to know, in order to put things right. I kind of think that we have to see the whole picture about what went wrong in order to see what we are fighting and make sure the same mistakes don't happen again."

"Guy, you are a wise young man and you are quite right. Education is hugely important. My grandfather knew Edward and held him in high esteem. They were great friends, although Edward was quite a bit younger than Grandpa. Edward set up his small community and that's where I met him. Grandpa tried to do what he could from the wider reaches of First City, and he fed vital information to Edward, but he had to be extremely cautious I think. In order to be able to provide information it was important that he didn't rock the boat. He and Granny talked to me about past events and I remember they stressed the importance of keeping a low profile, but being willing to help when called upon. I felt that some day I could perhaps make a difference. Not sure about that now."

"I think you could be a hugely influential character alongside us all," said Benedict, emerging with plates of poached salmon, new potatoes and salad.

What on earth could he have been doing in the kitchen all this time? thought Mystica.

"Now," said Benedict, " let's eat."

Chapter 20   Edward and Samuel

Samuel was in Ava's area, passing the time of day with one of his favourite people. He felt a strong connection to Ava, partly because she was Henny's mother and he felt that, in due course, he and Henny might make a good couple together. Henny was young, in her mid to late teens, and inclined to jump the gun over so many things, but she was a warm and loving personality. Her impetuosity was something that needed to be checked but he felt that she was learning from the mistakes and assumptions she had made; she was always full of remorse, and was utterly transparent in her feelings of regret and apology whenever she thought she had hurt someone.

"How is Henny feeling now?" he asked Ava. "Has she forgiven herself yet?"

"No, not really and I don't think she ever will, but she may be a bit more cautious in the way she wants to help people from now on. Philip has forgiven her, because he feels it was probably all his fault. It's that bit about him that is an incurable romantic I suppose."

"Pretty stupid really, having got that far away, with danger potentially lurking at every twist and turn, to try to go back. But, of course, Mystica could have stopped him from trying to return to us here for what was, in the end, just a toy. I know it was an important part of her past but, if blame has to be apportioned anywhere, she has to bear some of it herself. She probably should have just been disappointed and suggested that they carry on."

"That's what Edward told Philip, but it makes little difference to Philip's sense of loss in the long run."

"Well, Henny needs to be able to see that the whole thing was due to a set of circumstances and I'm happy to help in any way I can."

"Thank you Samuel. Your friendship means the world to her. I...I hope she doesn't get her hopes up too high. She is easily bruised."

"I shan't ever knowingly hurt her. I also have high hopes, and she figures in there very strongly. It's too soon now, but she is maturing. She certainly has some special qualities that I love. But she still needs to learn something more about controlling her impulses, without damaging her spontaneity. I hope I can help with that."

Ava walked over to him and gave him a hug. "You're a fine young man, Samuel, and we all have the utmost respect for you. Being able to trust people is what we're all about I guess, and we do have some wonderful people here who still need plenty of guidance."

At that point the door opened and Henny walked in.

"Talking about me, were you?"

"Absolutely, one hundred percent," replied Samuel. "What other topic of conversation could be as riveting?"

Henny laughed and subjected him to a playful punch in the stomach. He pretended to keel over and then caught her arm and twisted it neatly behind her back.

"Eeeow, stop!" she cried. "You'll break my arm!"

"Fat chance," he replied, but he let go and she went off into peals of laughter. Samuel felt a sense of relief hearing Henny's natural laughter taking over. She was healing. He realised then just how important that was to him.

"Actually," she said, "I've been looking for you. Edward asked me to find you. He wants to have a meeting with you in his secret garden, sort of now."

The artificial sunlight slowly curved its way across the walls, shattering into rainbow slices through the waterfall and into the pool. Edward was sitting by the side of the water, his eyes closed and his hands clasped as if in prayer. He looked up as Samuel went over to him and made to get up. Samuel gently pressed him back into the chair and seated himself on the low wall surrounding the pool.

"I've just been with Ava. Poor old Henny is still very much of the idea that she is to blame for the whole business of Mystica and the toy snow globe. I have said that I would help if it's possible. She needs to see that blame can't be apportioned for this in any one direction. Same with Philip I guess."

"You're right my boy. You have young shoulders but they already seem to carry much wisdom. I am sure you know that you are my chosen successor. The time isn't right for democratic elections as such, but I have already spoken to each of our friends in the community and the unanimous opinion is that I should ask you to take over the reins from me."

"But, Edward, I'm too young. I have no experience..."

"You have more experience than most and your years don't necessarily count as a requirement for perception and insight. You have the ability to see good sense, you don't make rash judgements, and people trust you. I was hoping that Mystica might have been able to help you, but I think you possess the understanding and knowledge necessary to carry things off on your own."

"I don't think I'm ready for this at all."

"Well, that's where your judgement is a trifle faulty, but at least it means you're not arrogant! Although, to a degree, you are right. And it's time to prepare you for what lies ahead. I am getting older and less able by the day. I am tired. I want you to take over and learn from me while there is still time. You must know that my days are numbered. However, we shall start from today and I will show you how to contact all the other small communities that make up our response to the High Council. All my files will be accessible to you and you will have some homework to do. First things first of course. Are you willing to be what I consider you are and have been for some time - the natural successor to me?"

"Well yes, but I thought this would be in the years to come. Not now. It is far too soon."

"There will never be the exact right moment, Samuel, so we have to engineer the situation. And there won't be years to come that we can wait for. Things happen when they happen and not necessarily when we plan for them to happen. I think you need to make a start on visiting the other small communities. I will prepare the way by introducing you distantly and we will make arrangements as to how to get you there."

"Should I go on my own or should someone come with me?"

"Who would you choose to take?"

"Well, if she were older, I would choose Henny. She needs a focus, something to replenish her self-esteem and I think it would be a good exercise for her, meeting people and learning the art of diplomacy and tact. But she is young, she might misinterpret the reasons for being asked to go. So I don't know really."

"I think you are right on all those counts. But there is a particularly good reason for her to go with you, and that will be revealed in due course."

Samuel looked at him with raised eyebrows.

"There are some loose ends to tie up first and I am not at liberty to tell anyone what they might be. All will be made clear sooner than expected I think. A journey with a purpose could be the making of her, but we have to be sure. Perhaps I'll have a word with her and see what I think before we make any decisions."

"That would be a great help. Then there would be no misunderstandings. Edward, I think I would like to make Henny my life partner. She and I have always had a special relationship and I'm probably not really that much older than her. But I worry about whether she will ever learn to control her spur of the moment decisions and actions. Is she irresponsible or just young? If she lacks judgement, that could present difficulties and, if I were to be in some position of authority, I don't know if they would be a barrier."

"I think you'll find that she learns quickly from her mistakes. Making mistakes and the importance of realisation is an essential part of education, of maturing. She feels her part in Mystica's disappearance keenly and she won't easily let go of that responsibility."

"We're both too young and I'm scared."

"Don't be. You will find you have all the strength you need and you won't be alone. Each of the outlying small communities have people with wisdom and experience and they will help you."

"I think I would like each of them to appoint a representative who I could call on and discuss things with on a regular basis, so that none of us feels isolated."

"A good plan. So far, with me leading things, our breakaway groups have been 'ruled' if you like by a benign despot, me! That was never the intention, but having just one person in authority seemed the best way forward at the beginning and things just haven't altered. It's time for a change. Each individual community has always been autonomous and that degree of independence has been important in helping to strengthen them and form robust loyalties. However, the time is approaching when the High Council and the regime in First City will need to be confronted and overturned. This is when the separate communities will need to join forces and be unanimous in deciding what the next steps will be."

"It sounds like a massive undertaking," said Samuel.

"It will be," replied Edward. "It will be the most important thing you will ever have done in your life, but you, and those chosen from each community to be the lead, will need plenty of time to plan with skill and precision. You will also have the great advantage of surprise when the time comes. Nobody in the High Council will be in the slightest bit aware of what is in the air. They have rested on their laurels for too long and they feel invincible. A great mistake."

"I don't know how to start."

"That's a good sign. You're wide open to advice!"

"But, how should I choose others to help?"

"The communities themselves will know who is best among them to take a lead. Within First City, as you know, we have our own network and they are recruiting more each day. These are people who are following the regime to the letter on the outside and building up valuable information in secret which is relayed to us on a regular basis. I shall give you the list of them all and details of how to contact them. One of the best is Kathleen, a great help to us."

"I know Kathleen," said Samuel. "I can't imagine she would ever be suspected of being other than a loyal stalwart First Citizen."

"Exactly so. Kathleen was Mystica's line manager in her office and appeared austere and inflexible. Mystica was very wary of her until she found out that Kathleen had been responsible for a letter urging her to leave her apartment. Mystica had no idea that the note had come from Kathleen and was astonished to learn that the very person she mistrusted was her salvation."

"Kathleen has some surprising qualities, by the sound of it."

"Well, Kathleen is pretty near top of my list for you. And now, to come to the subject of Mystica."

"Yes, poor Mystica. What a loss."

"Maybe."

Samuel looked puzzled.

"I have heard a rumour that Mystica may not have drowned after all, but is staying in one of the small outreach settlements. Word has it that she was washed up on a beach, with the help of a friendly dolphin I think, and is living with a family there who have been helping her to recover."

"Oh my God, that's fantastic," said Samuel. "We must go there as a matter of some priority and make sure she comes back safely."

"Well, I think we should bide our time a bit. I understand she has suffered significant memory loss. I feel she needs this to come back slowly and big shocks may be harmful."

"I see. But, should we tell Philip? I guess his reaction may be somewhat impulsive."

"For the moment, only you and I know. And it should stay that way."

"But, just a rumour you say? So it's not necessarily true."

"Well, it's a bit more than a rumour really, but I don't know what sort of state she is in so I'm keeping an open mind. My understanding is that she had virtually complete memory loss, but that things are beginning to emerge slowly, under the careful eye of the community medic. I know him. I remember him from his time here with us after his partner was taken for treatment. A lovely man called Benedict Eastman, and I think he will help Mystica to sort things out." Edward then looked rather thoughtful and frowned.

"What is it?" asked Samuel.

"Something, and maybe nothing," said Edward. "I think Philip needs to be involved in the way forward for First City, but there could be complications."

Samuel's training began in earnest and he spent each day learning about the resistance movement within First City. Kathleen came in to spend some time with him and she gave him all the relevant details of each of those opposed to the regime who were determined to do all that was necessary to overthrow the present system and restore things to some harmony. Kathleen had no desire to do anything other than continue in her present role as an undercover worker and actually seemed to revel in the duplicity! They talked about Lucas and Kathleen warned him to be careful. As she pointed out "Lucas is weak and could be a piece of flimsy straw in the breeze. On the other hand, he is partnered with a dangerous woman, and has an equally dangerous daughter. It would be useful to know what they are up to. I'll help if I can."

He learned about the various outreach communities, how to contact them and the names of key people. He started to make a journey plan but felt in his mind that he should try for one of the small outreach settlements first, a coastal settlement.

Chapter 21   Mystica and Benedict

"Dad told me the other day about some of the awful things that had happened in the past and how climate change and a virus had a catastrophic effect on life. Does that bring up any memories for you, Mystica?"

Guy was nothing, if not straightforward.

"Guy, these things may not yet be part of Mystica's recall. I'm not sure..."

"Oh, but they are," said Mystica. "Things that were vaguely in my consciousness a day or two ago are returning to me by the spadeful. This is all familiar territory, although it happened way before my time. And it is part of history that my grandparents told me about. So much of what happened in the past was the result of greed. After my parents' and grandparents' day, I was brought up to understand by the authorities that the only way to preserve life and improve the situation was to obey all rules without question. I am afraid that the idea of obeying without question is not in my nature."

"Was it always so dreadful?"

"I think things were fine to begin with and a certain optimism took hold, after all the dreadful events, wars, famine, floods, fires and so on. Everything had been rocketing out of control and it was time for strong management of the situation. "

"You're right," said Benedict. "It seemed as if, at last, something would be done to set the world straight, to stop man destroying humanity. The virus topped it all, such a small but deadly and invisible enemy. It was hardly spoken of, but people were shut away and given all that they needed individually to keep body (but not necessarily soul) alive. A strict regime was called for and, although it appeared harsh, it was as if an all-powerful father had set some new ground rules, stricter than anything seen before."

"But a strict regime turned into the harshest oppression and it wasn't long before people kicked back against it. They felt there had to be more to life than this. The virus had subsided, although it was always lurking in the background, so anyone who questioned the regime was taken to a 'hospital' and treated, if they hadn't fallen prey to the infection. This was a way of deterring others from disobeying the dictats and these people were treated as legitimate trial fodder to attempt to eradicate the epidemic. After all, everyone had enough to eat, everyone was warm and physically healthy, so anybody who created problems was seen as an enemy of the regime and had to be dealt with one way or another."

"That's true," said Benedict, "and, for some, it was soul-destroying."

"If you asked too many questions, you were immediately suspect. I know somebody who looked for more information ..."

Mystica broke off. The extent of her memory had almost been reached. She couldn't think who this person was, but she knew it made up the bit of memory that was perhaps the most painful missing part.

"Well, your own mother Guy..."

There was a sudden silence among that descended.

"I'm sorry. I didn't mean to bring things up that would spoil the party."

"No, you need to have the information. I started the ball rolling talking to you about it. You need to know what went wrong, in order to be part of change. Don't apologise."

"Your father's right, Guy. Our generation, but mainly yours probably, has the back-breaking task of achieving true recovery and none of us can even make a start without education. We do need to talk about it. We need to talk much more than we ever have and a place like this which is free from the cruelty and subjugation of the High Council, is the perfect place to start. On a lighter note, Ben, that was a wonderful meal. You are a fantastic chef. The salmon was perfect and I thoroughly enjoyed it. Thank you so much."

"Well, on that note," said Guy, "I will clear away and sort the dishes, while I think about how to save the world."

They all laughed, although the seriousness of his remark was not dismissed in any of their minds.

"You're obviously a good influence on my son," said Benedict, smiling at Mystica. "I can count the number of times he has done the clearing away on the fingers of one hand I think."

"Hey, watch it or I might change my mind."

Guy grinned but realised that his presence was not required, and watching his father take a more than platonic interest in Mystica was something he hadn't witnessed previously. The opportunity hadn't arisen before anyway, and he thought he should make himself scarce.

Mystica and Benedict went outside the housing unit that nestled in the hillside and took in the early evening air. They walked down to the beach. The sun was sinking below the hill on the other side of the estuary and it cast a shimmering golden pathway across the water. Behind them were sand dunes and, beyond the dunes, a dark wooded area. The air was calm and warm, with a gentle breeze wafting the sea grasses.

The only sounds were the grasses and the lapping of the sea on the outgoing tide, with the occasional cry of a seabird.

"Many years ago, there used to be a tiny church here, half buried in the sand dunes behind us," said Benedict.

"What happened? Where is it?" asked Mystica.

"All before my time. It was apparently destroyed and reduced to rubble. The stones were carted off somewhere and used for the hardcore foundations to some laboratory buildings miles away, or so I understand. Nobody came back here again. There were no houses left, no people. So, no life. Perfect for us."

"Oh yes, this is a perfect place. The air is so clear, so full of promise. There's so much sunlight and colour. That was what was missing in First City. There was no colour, no feeling of freedom. So many parts of my memory are coming back. There is still something important that is missing, but I feel free! I love it and feel very much at home here."

Mystica felt a warm contentment and something akin to happiness, although she felt she had no right to be cheerful, no entitlement to pleasure. But why not?

"I'm glad. It is a peaceful place and we have established a firm, dependable community. Long may it continue, but..."

"But what?"

"I feel that it is almost too idyllic. We know that things in First City have to change for a start, and the regime there has to be ousted. Small groups like ours are great, but everyone is entitled to a firm, strong government, without the corruption of the last years. You were right when you said that everything was fine to begin with, but how do we make changes without the same awful domination setting in? People in any position of power will demand an extra bite of the cherry for themselves if we aren't too careful. It's human nature and I'm afraid for the future. But we have to try."

Mystica felt troubled and a shadow crossed her face.

"I think this was part of the role that Edward had in mind for me in some way. A way in which I could help towards the future, bring about changes, ensure some peace and transparency of government. But you are right. People are naturally acquisitive and the damage done in the past will take a long time to heal. Your son is a lovely boy and will be a great asset to the system of government that we all need."

"I quite like him too!"

They walked down the beach and Benedict quite naturally took Mystica's hand. In his mind it was partly to prevent her falling, but it felt good to hold the hand of someone who had such an interesting character, who had the recovery of mankind in the core of her being. Mystica just accepted Ben's hand and rejoiced in its warmth and strength. Something at the back of her mind niggled a bit but she couldn't think what it was.

Chapter 22   Brooks, Henny and Ava

Samuel's training programme continued daily with Edward. He was quick to learn and commit names, contact details and useful information to memory. He to talked a lot to Henny, and discovered that not only did she have great artistic imagination and skill, but she also possessed a special affinity with people of all ages. The toddlers and babies in the nursery were always overjoyed to see her and the older folk looked forward to her transparent contentment and exuberance. Samuel grew closer to her day by day and looked out for her to chat, sometimes informally and sometimes discussing things on a more serious note to see what her reaction might be to different scenarios. If she thought it strange she didn't refer to it, but accepted that she was having her opinion sought because maybe she was maturing. She was flattered and took time these days to think carefully before she popped a random thought into the air. She was growing up. Samuel was increasingly sure of his decision to take her with him on his journeys to the smaller outreach communities, but kept that idea to himself.

Philip spent much of his time in design work for the unit. He oversaw the construction of new spaces for living quarters, paying special attention to light sources and the use of renewable energy. He also paid regular visits to the nursery section. His excuse was that he could see more of Louis but the truth was that he enjoyed the company of Lizzie and his feelings of guilt and sadness over the loss of Mystica were waning. Lizzie was in the nursery quarter on a daily basis and he found that, if for some reason she wasn't there when he visited, he was acutely disappointed. She was gentle and kind and Louis obviously adored her - that alone put her on a pretty high pedestal as far as Philip was concerned.

He also visited Brooks and helped in small ways in Brooks' work space. Brooks was still fairly silent, but always gave him something to do and they became strange friends, and Brooks even managed a smile now and then and a short sentence on occasions.

Philip liked Brooks. He liked the fact that Brooks passed no opinions and made no judgements. They could just go about things in a companionable silence. Now and then he took Louis into the workshop and Brooks seemed, at least, not to be averse to this young visitor. Louis smiled at him and called him "Boo". Brooks liked that. It was special.

One day Brooks paid a visit to the nursery section. He had never been before. He never left his workshop and living areas. But on this occasion he went in to the nursery. Evelyn showed no sign of this being an unusual occurrence. She smiled at him and welcomed him. Brooks looked at the murals that decorated the unit. He went up to the walls and touched the artwork, stroking it as if it was alive and would respond in some way. He let out a satisfying breath, and stood back from the wall, his face radiating a sort of sunshine.

"Boo!" a little voice called out and Louis lifted his arms up to Brooks. Brooks went over to him and gently touched him on his face, stroking him just as he had stroked the mural.

"Henny painted the walls," said Evelyn. "Lovely work she does. We're so pleased. She's very talented and we are reaping the benefit."

Brooks looked round at Henny and nodded. He then left the nursery section and returned to his own unit.

"Well now, that's a leap forward for Brooks," said Evelyn. "I think, I really think he is starting to make human contact again. That's the first time I have ever known him to leave his own sector, unless it is to do some sort of repair work. Amazing."

Henny had watched all this in astonishment. She had never really had anything to do with Brooks and like many small children, she had always been wary of him and kept her distance. It wasn't in her nature to be unkind, to poke fun or tease, but she didn't want to be alone with him, didn't really want to try and talk to him. However, she was starting to feel curious about this strange man.

"That was odd wasn't it? I mean, he never goes anywhere unless he really has to, in order to repair something. And Louis seems to know him quite well!"

"Philip has introduced Louis to him when he visited Brooks' workshop a few times and Brooks feels safe; he knows he is not in danger of teasing from very small children. Louis is wide open, warm and instantly friendly. Brooks would love that, I think."

"Tell me about him," asked Henny.

"I don't know much really. Your mother will be better able to answer questions I think."

Henny frowned and shrugged her shoulders.

"OK. Right. I'll get on with some overdue clearing out of the sandpit."

As she cleaned and organised the toys round the sand area, Henny couldn't quite get Brooks out of her mind. He had nodded to her after looking at the wall in a way that seemed to suggest some respect. She couldn't put it any other way, but it was odd. She knew, from Philip, that Brooks was artistic in his own right and she remembered Mystica talking about an extraordinary creative talent that she had detected in Brooks, over and above his mechanical and engineering skills. She had paid little attention at the time, seeing Brooks as just a kind of lonely old oddball.

As soon as she could, she went to the cleansing section and told her mother that it was time for a tea break. Ava raised her eyebrows, but said that she was ready for a breather and that everything was running on its usual automatic well-oiled wheels, so she could afford to sit and put her feet up.

"We had a visit in the nursery today, from Brooks of all people. It was extraordinary. He really seemed to like my painting. Didn't say anything, but somehow made it clear just by looking at me. He sort of nodded and then left. But Louis was delighted to see him, which was sweet."

"That's lovely," said Ava.

"So, Brooks. Tell me about him."

"Well, maybe at some point, but I don't know if this is the right time."

"What do you mean?"

"I don't know if Brooks' background should be, or needs to be, revealed."

"Well, he's an oddball, that's for sure and certainly spooky. He spooks me out. I always think he might be someone to avoid at all costs."

"No, he's not like that. He's had huge problems in his life I think."

"Well, how do you know? Is he a special friend of yours?"

"I really can't say too much, but he isn't unsafe in any way. He is someone to be pitied and helped."

"You pity him? Doesn't that make you a bit strange too perhaps? I mean he's not normal, is he?"

"Whatever that means."

"Good God Mum, he's a loony. I know he's good at fixing things, but he's just too weird for words. He's round the twist."

"Please don't say things like that. He is someone who is locked away inside himself. There, but for fortune, go any of us. We are the lucky ones. You don't know him. Don't judge him."

"Well, I'm certainly not going to befriend him, if that's what you want!"

"That is exactly what I would like, to tell you the truth."

"Fat chance!"

Ava took a deep breath.

"Brooks is your father."

"What?"

Henny was stunned, but waited for Ava to continue.

"We can't be related. We have absolutely nothing, not one thing, in common."

"You have more in common that you know, and I wish things were different so you could see that."

"He's not, he can't be. I don't want him to be my father! No way."

Henny got up and raced out of the cleansing section and into one of the long quiet corridors. She ran up the corridor to the end wall and sank down on her knees, leaning against the wall. She could feel hot, salty tears starting to course down her cheeks. She had no idea why she had been so rude and overbearing to her mother. Ava was her best friend and, as a mother, had given her undiluted love and protection always.

She didn't notice Philip coming towards her. He had seen her run from the meeting with Ava and had realised that something was wrong. He stood for a couple of seconds in front of her before she realised she wasn't alone.

"Oh God, Philip! I've been a cow. My mum is so lovely and I think I've hurt her, more than usual, this time."

"Do you want to talk about it?"

He slid down the wall and sat beside her on the floor.

"I was horrid about that daft old Brooks. And she was defending him. It got my goat and I sort of hit back. She said that he is my father. Can you believe that?"

Philip was silent for a moment.

"You know, that wouldn't surprise me in the least. Brooks is a remarkable person. You are both people with extraordinary talents. There's obviously more to all this than you know and, before you pass judgement, I think you should find out more information. If he is indeed your father, then you, of all people need to know and you need to know him."

"I'm too quick, too hasty. I guess my thoughtlessness was what got me into trouble with Mystica, making assumptions and thinking I was doing the right thing."

She burst into tears again. A fresh source of wretchedness overcame her.

"What shall I do?" she wailed.

"Go back to your Mum first. Apologise. Hug her. Ask to know more. She made a start and that can't have been easy after all these years. My guess is that only Edward knows about this, and now me of course, but my lips are sealed."

He helped her up and they slowly walked back to the cleansing unit. Philip left her at the doorway and she went in slowly. Ava was sitting in the same place, looking down at the floor, her arms drooping by her side.

"I'm so sorry, Mum. I really am. I wouldn't have hurt you for the world and I guess it wasn't easy telling me. And perhaps it wasn't easy in those early days with Brooks either. I'm such a witch."

Ava slowly lifted her head and smiled gently at Henny. Her eyes were wet and Henny realised she had reduced her mother to tears.

"Sorry, sorry, sorry!" whispered Henny and gave her mother the biggest hug, short of crushing her ribs, that was possible.

"Please tell me more. I need to understand. I need to know."

"We were partnered in the First City regime. He was an inventive, imaginative person and that, thankfully, has never left him. In our own way, we discovered a sort of contentment in each other's company, a gentle love. He never talked much but what he had to say was always just right. We were quiet and caused no ripples. We were seen as a perfect match. We would produce a quiet child. We would be no trouble. Jules, his name is Julian, like all creative and scientific people, had an enquiring mind that never stopped. For the most part he took care that when he was making discoveries he was not seen. However, his covert activities brought him to the attention of the authorities and he was hauled away one day. They gave him some peripheral, minor treatment that removed a lot of his memory and thought that had done the trick. He didn't recognise me, although somehow he found his way back to our apartment."

"Where was I?"

"You were just a baby at the time, but he didn't recognise you either. He had been a warm, loving father and it chewed me to pieces to see that he had no interest in you any more. You were a stranger. He took no notice of you."

Henny sighed.

"That's awful."

"We couldn't really go on like that, but he wandered the streets and was taken in by one of Edward's people and looked after gently and carefully. He was able to carry out a narrow, repetitive range of activities but possessed great imagination and was always very creative. That had never left him, although in reality it was the very thing the authorities had wanted to destroy. Jules had withdrawn into some confused shadowland; life, as he had known it, had spun out of control and he had retreated into where he had been as a child, somewhere, I think, on the autistic spectrum. I followed him, with you, and we were all three taken into the community. My skills at housekeeping were luckily just what were required and you grew into the life of the community and remembered nothing of your babyhood. However, Jules only communicates with me on a minimum level where he has to and still shows no real recognition. He answers only to the name of Brooks."

"That's shattering. Poor Brooks. Poor Julian. Poor Dad. What can I do?"

"Be kind."

Henny squeezed Ava's arm and nodded.

"There is one more thing. One more important thing. When you were born, you had a twin brother. Jules and I had known that I was expecting twins and that this was not allowed. We had a hard decision to make, but we needed to ensure that you both had a life, a future."

"Oh my God, this is unreal."

"We agreed with a young couple we had somehow got to know, and felt we could trust, that they would take the twin who arrived second, whether boy or girl. It didn't matter to them - they seemed unable to have a child and were desolate. Somehow we felt we were helping both families to some sort of life within the regime. It was all a bit of a lottery, but the situation was serious. The authorities would have found out that I had given birth to twins and the likelihood was that we would have lost you both. We had no choice."

"Then, I have a brother somewhere. But where?"

"I don't know, but my understanding is that he and his family are safe and well. They live in one of the small communities on the outer fringes of the unknown territory - that's what the High Council used to call anywhere outside First City, in an attempt to make it sound forbidding I think."

"And I now have a father as well, even if part of him is somewhat absent."

Ava smiled.

"We have to be patient. I think he is starting to climb out of the perplexing and complex part of his nature. He has resisted returning to us deliberately sometimes, through being afraid and his defensiveness has made it difficult to break through, but Mystica made a start on that, and Philip and Louis are finding ways to create a crack in his armour, and I do so much want him back."

"It's strange that he doesn't acknowledge you of all people."

"Not really. I think he is terrified that he will be hurt again, perhaps taken away, or that I will be taken away. It was such an appalling time and he doesn't want to go through that again. So I remain patient. But you, you could make a difference. He wouldn't associate you with removal and treatment."

"I'm so glad you told me. I'll make friends with Brooks, Dad, somehow."

"Take it a step at a time and you may have to take your lead from him. He has already shown you that he has noticed and appreciated your artwork. That's a good start. But don't be in too much of a hurry, take your time, let him take his time."

In the meantime, Philip had gone to visit Brooks, with Louis, and with an excuse that Louis's rainbow lights were not functioning properly. The rainbow lights were Brooks' invention and they proliferated across the ceiling of Louis's bed section. He loved the coloured lights that changed slowly and spread themselves in never-ending rainbow streaks, decreasing their hue gradually in proportion to Louis's sleepiness, turning off eventually when the boy was asleep.

Brooks said he would check the connection remotely and, if all was still not working properly, he would call in and check the in situ connections.

"Boo!" Louis grinned and put out his hand to Brooks.

Brooks tentatively took it and held it gently, stroking the soft skin.

"Lou!" he said and Philip laughed. Philip had never heard Brooks come anywhere close to a non-serious exclamation, an intimate sort of joke.

"Thanks, Brooks, that would be great. By the way, I understand you were visiting the nursery earlier."

Brooks frowned slightly, as if he had been caught out doing something objectionable or improper.

"I was so pleased," said Philip quickly. "My boy tells me everything you know. No secrets from him. When I went to see him a while ago, the first thing he said was 'Brooks!' so there we are." Brooks looked relieved and a faint smile crossed his face.

"I gather you liked young Henny's art work. She's extraordinary and I just love her imagination and her use of colour."

"Interesting. Talented, yes. I like it."

"Having had some tiny bit of artistic training I do cast a critical eye over her stuff from time to time, but I am a poor substitute for someone who has a wonderful natural talent like you."

"I had no training."

"Well I guess if you're a genius you don't need it! I'm sure she'd love it if you took a look at some of her other work. It's nearly all mural activity and she perhaps ought to think about doing some watercolour pictures, or oil or pastel work. Whatever. Anyway, I think you'd been doing her a great favour if you had a peep at what she does. Perhaps you could guide her a bit. Don't know really, but she's a lovely girl. Has a few problems and, like all of us, deserves a bit of support from someone who knows what makes painting tick!"

Brooks was not someone to wait. He was obsessional to an overwhelmingly large degree and, having decided that he wanted to do just what Philip suggested, he left his workshop as soon as Philip and

Louis had gone. He made his way to the small recreation room where he knew Henny was redecorating one wall. The room was empty, so he could spend as much time as he wanted studying the painting. He had, of course, seen her painting before, but he was always in a hurry to go from one place to another and never stopped to take a close look. This was the first time that he had been still long enough to study what was in front of him. She had sketched out some imaginative coastal scenes and made a start on the painting. He realised she had never seen the ocean or a beach or seabirds, but somehow it was all there. He was enthralled by what he saw and delighted in the first splashes of colour that she had used.

He didn't notice Henny coming in and standing next to him. Ava had come with her to look at the work in progress, but stayed by the doorway while Henny went on in. Henny was amazed that he was there, but determined to treat it as a normal situation.

"So what do you think?" she asked gently.

"Oh. Talented. You've got it. Must go."

"Thanks, but please don't rush off. What do you think about my colour? Is it too rough, too crude, too 'edgy'?" She was afraid for a moment that she was being too pushy and that he might be frightened off.

"Don't know what that means. It's perfect. Perfection can always be perfected, of course, and you will do better things."

"That's the nicest thing anyone's ever said to me."

And, thought Henny, I bet that's one of the longest sentences you've spoken to anybody in a century.

Henny looked at Brooks and saw the glimmerings of a familial recognition cross his face. She also felt a recognition of what she already knew and they smiled at each other.

"I'll come tomorrow with a present for you," said Brooks.

Henny touched him lightly on the arm and nodded her thanks. Ava was thrilled to see that they were tentatively making a relationship of sorts.

Chapter 23   Edward and Henny

Brooks turned and left the recreation room. Ava had walked away first. She didn't want to spoil what was, for the pair of them, a personal and very special time. She felt the glimmerings of hope for Henny, for Brooks and, ultimately, for her.

After Brooks had left, Henny felt pleased with the encounter and determined to work at the relationship that she had only just discovered. She knew she would have to practise the utmost care and tact dealing with Brooks. It would be, for her, a true test of how mature and prudent she could be. She knew she had a lot to learn and wanted, so much, to be in possession of good judgement.

She decided that she needed to talk to Edward and went to his quarters to see if he would have a moment or two to spare.

She knocked gently on his outer door and went in, without waiting for a response. This was usual and he always welcomed spur-of-the-moment visits. These were usually the times when people most wanted and needed to open their hearts to him.

Henny looked across to Edward's chair and saw that he was fast asleep. It was unlike him to take naps, and she didn't like to wake him, but she so much needed to offload some thoughts and feelings. She touched him gently on his sleeve and his eyes slowly opened. He smiled and sat up.

"Must have dropped off. Henny, what a delight to see you. I have you on my list to pay you and your paintings a visit, but you've got to me first!"

Henny looked at his face, more lined and tired than she had ever noticed before and was alarmed. Suddenly she was aware of his mortality. He wasn't going to be with them forever. She was distressed and her expression must have given away her feelings.

"You are certainly looking at a tired old man, my dear. But don't be troubled. Things are in place for when I must finally go, and leave you all I must in due course! It is the order of things. But now, is there a special reason why you have come to see me?"

"It's Brooks."

"Ah, so Ava and you have been talking."

"He's my father."

"And a better, nicer, gentler man for a father couldn't be wished for."

Henny looked puzzled.

"He has some major part of himself still rather locked up, but it is unravelling bit by bit. Mystica was a good friend to him in the short while she was here and Philip has tried to continue that, with Louis. However, he needs to know you. He needs to see how you are so much a part of him, a part that he can be proud of. And he will be proud of you I am sure. He needs to acknowledge you as his daughter."

"I had a big argument with my mother and said some pretty awful things. I'm so impulsive and I hate myself for it, but I apologised and she told me all the background to Brooks, my Dad's, treatment. It is so awful and I felt miserable at having said some unkind things about him. Then he came to see me in the small recreation room, where I'm doing my sea picture. He didn't say much, but I got the feeling of someone who is so powerfully creative, someone I so much want to be close to."

"And you will, in time. He needs a lot of love, some unconditional friendship and an enormous amount of patience."

"Why doesn't he recognise my mother?"

"I think he does, deep down, but there is the fear inside him that because something he was so deeply involved with was taken away from him, it might happen again. Better not to have such an intimate relationship, better not to hurt or be hurt like that again. It will be easier for him to come to terms with you first, one stage removed, and then in time I am sure that he and Ava will be reunited."

"I do hope so. I've only just come to realise what an incredible and complex person he is. I really want him to be part of our family. And then, there's my brother..."

"Yes, poor Ava and Julian had to make a tough decision, but it was the right one."

"Do you know where he is? Could I find him perhaps?"

"Anything's possible, but you would have to be sure not to rock somebody else's boat. He is, after all, part of someone else's family and always has been as far as he is concerned. Your diplomatic skills will be tested to the utmost if you come across him. He may not know the circumstances of his birth."

"That's true. I hadn't thought of that. I just sort of assumed that he would obviously be just as curious about me as I am about him. I would have to be careful."

"Henny, there are some important changes that are being planned for the near future and I am likely to call a community meeting very soon. Samuel knows about this, as he has to. It's never been much of a secret that he is my chosen successor and I have been preparing him for this for quite a while. This has stepped up in intensity just recently, because I need him to know as much as possible in what might be a smaller amount of time than I had foreseen."

"But you're not ill are you, Edward? You're OK?"
Edward smiled at Henny's anxious face.

"Henny, I am an old man and I'm tired. Anything could happen at any time and I want to ensure that we are in the safest of hands for the future. I haven't mentioned any of this to anyone else. No, I am not ill, but I can't go on much longer and I need someone I can trust to take over. Samuel is my gift to you all. There is an important route being mapped out for you also at the moment but that is for Samuel to talk to you about, not me. There now, I am as indiscreet as anybody. I should have kept my mouth shut!"

He chuckled.

"I shan't say anything, and I promise you I won't let you down. I shall work hard on my assumptions and my lack of tact."

"I know you will. And promise me you will never lose your marvellous spontaneity!"

"I love you Edward, and I promise."

Chapter 24   Polly and Phoebe

Polly and Phoebe had become more secretive than ever and discussed things quietly between themselves. Whenever Lucas entered the room they immediately became silent.

However, Lucas was as determined as he could be to make things look as though he was co-operating. It was important to him to find out as much information as possible that might be of some use to Edward and he persisted in being helpful round the apartment, making meals, ensuring everywhere was clean and tidy. Polly hadn't made the mistake of leaving her notebook anywhere around for him to find, so he had to try and catch smidgens of conversation between the two of them.

"Anything interesting happen today?" he asked.

They looked at him in astonishment.

"Just making conversation. We don't do that much do we?" said Lucas, trying to make light of it.

"Can't think why my mother should tell you anything. You are hardly a true respecter of the regime, are you?" said Phoebe.

"Phoebe, I am trying to make amends for possibly not being the most supportive partner. Not that it is anything that should concern you."

"Everything concerns me. Far more than it has ever concerned you. Who are you? You're not important. You're pretty much a nobody, especially where the authorities are concerned. I despise you!"

"Polly, are you going to let Phoebe talk to me like that? I know we have had our differences, but I would appreciate your support in ensuring that Phoebe doesn't talk to me in that way."

Polly laughed and Phoebe just smiled and left the room.

"How can I chastise her for being truthful? You are weak Lucas, and you've always been spineless. Phoebe just sees what is there."

Lucas said nothing for a minute or two.

"So, anything worthy of note happening then? I am trying to show my interest and doing my best to be supportive."

"Worthy of note? What do you mean?" asked Polly. "My work is not open to discussion. It is highly restricted information."

"And yet, Phoebe seems to have your confidence. Your daughter, but not your partner."

"Lucas, since honesty is the order of the day, I have to say that I wish you had never been my partner and, although it isn't in my remit to criticise the authorities, this was obviously the one giant mistake they had made."

"Polly, whatever you may think of me, you should support me where Phoebe is concerned. I know nothing about adolescent girls, but I know they can be difficult and rude. However, I'd like to be able to have a friendly relationship with my daughter."

She smiled. "Your daughter?" leaving it to him to decipher what exactly that might mean.

Lucas let out a long deep breath. He accepted, with great relief, that perhaps Polly had been unfaithful and that, therefore, Phoebe may not have been related to him at all. Thank heavens he could loathe the child without feeling guilty that he was repulsed by his own daughter.

He appreciated that Polly was perhaps not perfect in the eyes of the authorities. For her part, Polly realised that Lucas might now have a kind of hold over her and could denounce her and Phoebe at some point. Perhaps he was, even now, establishing his own list of her transgressions, starting with adultery.

"Lucas, you had better watch your step. Phoebe and I have been noticing that your friendships with local people are suspicious and open to scrutiny and question."

"I assure you I have no friends."

"Well, I can probably believe that."

"And the last thing on my mind would be to go to the authorities and upset the family applecart."

"Well, no," she said. "I might well get there first. I find you objectionable and you may as well know that I have always disliked you. We really have no relationship worth saving."

But, of course, partnerings do not readily get dissolved and Lucas realised that the situation was serious for him. He now knew that his time was limited and he realised he had to make contact with Edward and his followers, to save his sanity, if not his life. He sat and pondered on this while Polly left the room, preparing to go out to one of the Observer meetings.

It became obvious to him that the difficult time they had just spent was going to result in Polly deciding to denounce him straight away. He had done a poor job at trying to convince Polly that he was going to support her.

Chapter 25   Lucas

Polly and Phoebe left the apartment block without a word to Lucas, slamming the door behind them. In the stillness there was the small sound of the electrical system ticking gently away in the background. Usually a friendly sound, today it seemed threatening and Lucas knew it was time to leave. Part of him was sustained by having made the decision to go; but a large portion of fear and anxiety gripped him. He felt a wave of nausea slither across his belly and a quickening of his heartbeat. However, his mind was unwavering and he knew he had reached the point of no return. There was no other choice in front of him.

He made his way out of the apartment, taking nothing with him. He had few possessions really and wanted nothing with him to remind him of his bitter partnership with Polly, or the enduring contempt in which he was held by Phoebe.

He travelled through the cold, grimy streets, glad that they were empty, keeping himself close to the walls. The one thing that lifted his spirits was the thought that Edward and his group would take him in and he would be sheltered. He didn't know what he might be able to offer them. He had no skills, no particular talent; he was, as Phoebe had said, "pretty much a nobody". Perhaps Edward would turn him away. He looked everywhere for a red silk handkerchief sticking out of a pocket - Samuel's signature - but he was alone on the street. His footsteps seemed to echo along the pavement, however hard he tried to move without a sound, and he kept looking round, partly to check that he wasn't being followed and partly in the hope that Samuel was going to appear. He was dismayed to find he was unsure about the direction he was going in. Was he travelling further from Edward's community? Was he moving closer to danger? Each street, every wall, and all the anonymous buildings looked the same. He was confused but had to continue and hope he was on the right track.

From a careful distance Samuel saw him and watched as Lucas, furtively, moved forward towards the community but he looked guilty and this made him decidedly conspicuous. His way of keeping close to the wall, of looking round constantly and keeping his head down, was strikingly prominent. He was certainly going in the right direction, and was quite close to the community, but his eye-catching progress made Samuel worry that Lucas's activity might endanger them all. It was a relief to Samuel when he realised that Lucas had no real idea of just how close he was to his target destination. That much was clear. Samuel stayed still and silent in the shadows and watched, while deciding how soon, or even if, he should approach Lucas.

Lucas stopped and looked around him, trying to remember some point of reference from when he had been this way before. But it was hopeless. Everything was undistinguished, unidentifiable. The shadowy parts near the wall were dull and, although they may have held secrets of their own, they revealed nothing. Lucas was bewildered and afraid and started to move more into the open to get a clearer idea, as he thought, of his location.

Samuel had a worrying feeling that something was wrong; he held back and continued to monitor the situation and just wait. He had noticed two faceless and rather ordinary-looking men also lurking in the shadows, watching Lucas carefully. Lucas had thrown caution to the wind and had stepped off the pavement looking all round, trying to find his bearings, trying to get some sense of locality. Samuel watched and waited. He was uncomfortable and concerned that these men, as well as Lucas, were in close proximity to his community unit.
It became apparent that the two men were in no way interested in anything, or anybody, other than Lucas. They presumably had no idea that Samuel and his friends were so close, or even existed. Just the thickness of a couple of walls separated Edward's group from the grim reality of First City.

Some words were exchanged and a look of resignation appeared on Lucas's face as he was led away gently, but firmly. He had no strength or ability to fight back and it would have been hopeless had he tried.

Samuel was relieved to see Lucas being persuaded to go with the men and he exhaled a sigh of relief. He hoped that Lucas was able to keep the existence of Edward's community to himself. He felt somehow that, although they were more vulnerable than they had ever been, Lucas did have some ability to keep that knowledge to himself. If so, they were safe for now. But for how long? And if not, they would need to keep themselves well concealed. Fortunately, it had looked fairly clear that Lucas had little idea of how to reach the community but, if he were to be tortured, the sheer agony of physical torment might be enough to make him talk, and whatever he might say could lead to a massive hunt. They would need to be well prepared. When he was sure the coast was clear, Samuel slid quietly and cautiously into the shadows of a narrow alleyway and made his way immediately to Edward's quarters.

"We may have some major problems ahead," he said to Edward. "Lucas couldn't find the way to our access point. It was just as well he was blindfolded when he visited us before, both when he arrived and left but, by sheer chance, he was closer than he realised."

"I suppose it might have been something relatively innocent," said Edward. "It may have been a minor transgression; it may have been that he was just straying a little further than they would like and perhaps they will just give him a bit of a wigging and tell him to behave in future. He might tell them he was trying to gather information to pass on."

"Perhaps," Samuel said doubtfully.

Lucas had been taken, in silence, to one of the authority's interrogation rooms. There was a glass panel, with mirrored glass on one side and the capacity to observe from the other. Polly sat behind this glass and was joined by Kathleen. They greeted each other with a nod and Kathleen noticed Polly had a somewhat self-satisfied smug look on her face. She herself kept her features expressionless and turned to face the glass. Kathleen had been Mystica's line manager and Mystica had been very wary of her. She always appeared harsh and rigid and Mystica felt a necessity, at all times, to keep a very low profile. She didn't cause too many flutterings at any time and thought that she had gone pretty well unnoticed. However, Kathleen, for all her strict adherence to the High Council's policies, was a counter-Observer, reporting back to Edward and the community. She had been instrumental in warning Mystica and Philip when the time was right for them to leave First City and seek the sanctuary that they found in Edward's community. Her great gift to the local hidden community was that she was careful, at all times, to show no emotion, to appear utterly loyal to the regime and was considered one of their most trustworthy people.

Lucas was questioned about why he was wandering the streets at the limit of the First City boundary.

"What were you doing there, Lucas?" asked a gentle-faced man, who looked as if the whole thing was a bit tiresome, but nothing more.

"I was just trying to get a feel for the outer parts of the city, in case anything became apparent," replied Lucas. He realised this sounded feeble, but couldn't think of anything to add.

"What kind of thing were you looking for, Lucas?"
"I don't really know."
"That's a bit pathetic, Lucas, don't you agree?"
"I was just trying to see if I could be more reliable as an assistant to my partner, Polly."
"In what way more reliable?"
"I don't really know."
"You don't really know anything do you?"
"No."
"I think we need to encourage you a little to dredge through that rather ineffectual little mind of yours and see what you really do know that might help us. What do you think?"
"I'm sure I can't help you yet, but I could if you let me walk the streets a bit more. I'm sure..."

"No, that's a bit unconvincing, Lucas. I think you need a little help. We'll talk again later."

He smiled almost tenderly and touched Lucas gently on the arm. He motioned Lucas to stand, the door opened and he was led away.

Polly exhaled deeply with a look of satisfaction on her face.

"He's always been a burden, never a help, always shabby and useless. Phoebe and I are better off without him and we can get on with our observations without having to think about him."

Kathleen nodded and left the room. She had been there to verify to the authorities that no undue force of harshness was apparent in the interrogation. She could do that and find out what was likely to happen to Lucas next. Polly was pleased that her co-observer for Lucas's interrogation was Kathleen. She knew her to be a completely dedicated and honourable member of the regime and she was flattered that Kathleen had been chosen to be there.

Kathleen left the interrogation unit and returned to her office. She had a covert messaging system which relayed to Edward alone. It had been developed by Brooks and was highly sophisticated.

"Lucas has been taken for further questioning. I guess persuasion is a strong option on the cards, but I get the feeling that he will remain stubbornly silent. Treatment of some sort is bound to follow."

She sent her message to Edward.

Hours later Samuel carefully made his way further into First City. This was something he did on rare occasions as it was a potential danger zone for him and for the community. However, a second message from Kathleen reported that Lucas had been released and was wandering the streets aimlessly, his thought processes having been 'rearranged' in some way. Dreadful for him, but also stupidly useless to the authorities - a gesture to others perhaps and that was all. Samuel came across him wandering not far from the interrogation building. The street was empty with the exception of a few workers who hurried past Lucas, paying no attention to him, afraid for themselves if they showed any signs of friendship or pity. Samuel also paid little attention to him, but he was used to scrutinising people while appearing to disregard them totally.

Lucas's eyes were dull and unresponsive. He didn't recognise Samuel and made no attempt to talk to him. It was clear that he had been treated. Samuel made his way back to the community cautiously, keeping an eye open at all times for anyone who might be watching him.

"I feel a great sense of guilt always for those who I don't manage to help," said Edward. "I could have taken Lucas in before, but I thought he could be of great benefit to us on the outside. I was wrong. He wasn't strong enough."

"We can't help everybody," said Samuel.

"No, but we can try. And I made a mistake."

"Lucas was a sad individual," said Samuel. "He was always destined to be one of life's distressing losers."

"That's not a good enough reason to deny him what we all have, but I made a mistake. A good lesson for you Samuel I think. We do make mistakes. You will make mistakes. But you must always be prepared to acknowledge them and to learn from your mistakes. I am still learning from mine."

"I'm sure to make many and I hope I learn! One thing that has emerged from this, Edward, is that we are more vulnerable here than we thought. We mustn't be complacent. Perhaps now is the time to think about how we go on from here."

"I have been pondering this for a little while and the time is arriving when we need to move out a bit further and establish ourselves in a new location, or join forces with one of the other outreach communities."

"But we need to be close at hand to keep a convenient eye on what is going on in First City don't we?"

"My idea would be to retain this unit, as it is close to First City, to be a command post, a place where operations could be coordinated from. We will need a small trained group of people to operate it and report back. Someone will need to be in charge - not you, since you have to keep the overall wider brief going - and we may need to think about that pretty soon."

Chapter 26   Marnie, Joseph and Torrey

News items were infrequent from the First City community, and indeed rare between the outreach groups. They all tended to live as fairly autonomous population units, although from the very beginning it was clearly understood that such self-sufficiency was likely to be a relatively temporary thing. When the time was right to overthrow the regime, it would be necessary to unite and work in solidarity. Edward had let things slip a little as time had gone on, partly because he had concentrated on how things were within First City itself, how the regime was working and whether there were loopholes which would allow the High Council to be removed from power. He was also tired and old. He didn't have the physical stamina that he had had in the beginning and, in spite of his perception, his experience and his wisdom, he was in danger of losing his powers of observation. However, it was clear that the units beyond First City needed to be instructed and guided, and he needed to set that in motion. Each unit had to be prepared and communication between them all was going to be vital.

In the Seadrift community, Benedict was the co-ordinator of information from First City. So far, news had been sporadic but he knew he needed to get in touch to let them know about Mystica. It was obvious that First City had been her home, but what her intention had been in leaving and how she had arrived on their shores remained a mystery. He realised that he had to find out, but he felt an element of reluctance about the whole thing. He had grown to care for her, he took a delight in her company and was in no way eager for that to be taken away from him. He could sense that she had developed an affection towards both him and Guy; these feelings of tenderness between them fulfilled something that had been missing for them both, but he knew in his heart that maybe the gentle love that was growing might be too soon for Mystica. He needed to hold back and perhaps let Mystica take the lead.

However reluctant Benedict was to discover the truth about Mystica, he knew it was only fair to her that he should get in touch with Edward and let him know that she was safe. Brooks had devised some secure contact channels, which were not used too often between First City and the other communities. However, Benedict opened communications and Edward was quick to respond. Benedict told him about Mystica and Edward said that he had heard about the possibility of Mystica having survived. Benedict told him that Mystica had a significant memory loss, but that her recollections were gradually returning. She remembered Edward clearly, but her recalls in general were taking their time. Benedict said what a wonderful person Mystica was and how much they seemed to have in common. Everyone had warmed to her.

It was clear to Edward that Benedict's own feelings had been well and truly taken over. He did not mention Philip, having noticed a growing friendship between Philip and Lizzie. This created a complication and it was hard to know what to do. His experience of love and relationships was not huge and he felt it best to see how things "panned out". He simply told Benedict that Samuel would be making a journey to meet the other units and he would ensure that Samuel knew in advance about Mystica. Things would have to progress slowly; the knowledge that Philip was alive and safe would be a shock once she remembered who Philip was. However, remembering Philip had to come first, and it was clear that difficult choices would have to be made.

Edward also told Benedict about Henny and her twin brother. Henny would be travelling with Samuel and he needed Benedict to know this. Benedict had some background information and, of course, he instantly knew who Henny's brother was. He agreed to pave the way. This would be an interesting family relationship to be unpicked for the twin brother and he hoped it wouldn't spoil the wonderfully firm bond that had always existed between the children and the parents. It was the time for hard decisions to be made and transparency was the order of the day. It hadn't seemed to matter before, when it looked unlikely that paths would cross, but now...

Benedict made his way to the Baxters' unit and passed his hand across the doorway. The door slid open silently and Ben caught the whiff of something warm and home-baked.

"Wow, that smells really wonderful!" he said.

"Mystica has made us blueberry muffins," said Juno. "Can't wait to get my teeth into them, but I promised I'd take Mystica to the old church site and Torrey is already there looking for any useful pieces of wood he can pick up and use. The muffins will be cool enough to eat when we get back. Or did you want one of us, like Mystica perhaps?" She shot a rather bogusly naive grin at him and darted out of the door.

Mystica smiled at him, shrugging her shoulders in an embarrassed apology, and he chuckled. She followed after Juno.

"Tea, Benedict? Or coffee?"

"Thanks Marnie. Coffee would be great. It's you and Joseph I came to see actually and I wanted to see you on your own. I've been talking to Edward today and things are beginning to hot up somewhat in First City. He feels that the time is coming when we all need to be prepared to band together and oust the old regime. We have a lot of preparation work to do first and each community unit has to be ready to work as one. In the meantime, Edward's proposed successor, Samuel, will be taking time out to visit us all. He is young, but Edward feels he has a wisdom and perception beyond his years and will lead well. He is bringing his chosen partner with him, Henny."
Benedict looked carefully at both Joseph and Marnie. Marnie drew in a sharp breath and Joseph looked straight ahead at the wall.

"I remember Brooks and Ava, and little Henny of course. Torrey doesn't know," she said. "We've never felt we needed to tell him, never thought the occasion would arise to make it necessary. He has always been our 'first-born' if you like because, when we thought we couldn't have children of our own, along came Juno. "

"I guessed as much. Torrey has the colouring of his natural mother and in no way resembles either of you. He could have been an interesting throwback, but of course I knew Ava and I knew Brooks. It was pretty easy to put two and two together."

"So, what do we do?" asked Joseph.

"You will need to tell him."

"Of course. That won't be easy," said Marnie.

"Look, you have always been wonderful parents to both Torrey and Juno. You have nothing to reproach yourselves about, and I am sure he will understand. It will be a shock, but I think he has enough perception and judgement to be able to see the reality of the situation and the sensitivity to cling to the wonderful love you have always had for him. He will also understand the compassion you demonstrated to Ava and Brooks when they had to make a hard choice. Juno needs to know as well and she will be just as stunned. Total openness is needed with them both and, if you want my help, just let me know."

Juno, Torrey and Mystica returned, bringing with them a large piece of driftwood.

"Can that please stay outside?" asked Marnie. "There's no room for it here and it's soaking wet."

"Yep," said Torrey. "I'll need to cover it with something until it dries out. Then I'll be able to work on it."

"What are you going to do with it?" asked Benedict.

"That's what we wanted to know," said Juno. "He hasn't a clue!"

"Not yet, but it is just such a wonderful shape and I love it."

"Mouse liked it too," said Juno.

"It's not for dogs. I'll find something to make out of it. Or not. I might just let it be what it is," said Torrey, his eyes shining with excitement.

That's the artist, thought Benedict.

"Mystica, do you feel like another walk round to our place? A glass of wine with Guy and me perhaps? I need to talk about some aspects of your recovery before you put in some hard physical work helping Joseph with the farming!"

"I'd love to. Thanks. Is that OK Marnie? Anything you would like me to do to help with the meal?"

"No thanks. It's all sorted. Joseph and I need a little time with the kids as a matter of fact."

"Oh God yes, I'm so sorry. I should have realised. Of course you do. I'll make myself scarce and annoy Benedict and Guy instead!"

"No, no," said Marnie. "I didn't mean that at all. You are like one of the family, but there is something that Joseph and I need to discuss with Torrey and Juno and I don't think it can wait."

"Sounds ominous," said Juno.

"Not really..." said Joseph, "but let's get a drink as well. Benedict had the right idea. I think the sun is almost past the yardarm."

Benedict and Mystica left the Baxters' unit and Benedict reached gently for Mystica's arm.

"So, what's up?" said Torrey.

"It's not too easy to know where to start," said Marnie, "but I think we need to plough straight in."

She told them both in warm, affectionate terms how Torrey was not their natural son, but that he had been offered as a special gift to them to be their child when it was thought that childbirth for Marnie was not possible. His natural parents had produced twins and in First City only one child was allowed to each partnership. If Torrey hadn't been given to them he would have been taken away and it was impossible to predict what would have happened next.

Torrey and Juno looked at their parents and then at each other in astonishment.

Joseph continued. "By some strange quirk of nature, your mother became pregnant and Juno was the result. So we were then a wonderful family of four."

"Why have you never told us before?" asked Torrey.

"It never seemed important."

"Not important?" said Torrey. "Not important to you or me or who?"

"I mean," said Marnie, "that as far as we were concerned you were as natural born a child as we could ever hope for. You were our son, the first born, although not to us. We were moving from First City and there was no reason why you would ever meet your natural mother. She had to make the most difficult decision in her life, to give up one child to save both of them and she did this with the most selfless love that anyone could ever express. We promised that we would tell you about her, and about your birth, when the time was right."

"It seems to have taken a long time," said Juno.

"Yes," said Joseph. "And maybe we should have spoken sooner, but it never seemed quite the right moment."

"I don't know what to say," said Torrey. "It's a bit of a kick in the teeth I suppose, and I ought to feel devastated. But somehow, I don't. I have never felt anything other than complete love from you."

"That, my darling boy, has never ever been in question."

"But I have always thought there was something different about me, as if I didn't quite fit the mould. I would never have been able to describe it and, in an odd way, it's a bit of a relief. I think looking in the mirror each day told me something was a bit off beam. My eyes are so different from yours - all of you - and you can tell a lot from eyes. So, here we are then..."

"But why now?" asked Juno. "Waiting so long is one question that hasn't really been answered but maybe we would all do things the same way. But why tell Torrey now?"

"Because the time is approaching when things are likely to need further changes and the likelihood is that you may well meet up with your natural twin sister in the course of this."

"What changes? What's happening? I'm scared!"

"Don't be," said Joseph. "It has been apparent for a few years that the regime in First City has become increasingly corrupt and plans have been set for the outreach communities to depose the regime and establish a regular, efficient governing body based on honesty and integrity. "

"It will all take a bit of time and it has to succeed straight away," said Marnie. "There's no room for errors. All the outlying communities have to be in full agreement."

"One further thing is that Mystica has remembered things about First City and people she has met. You may remember us telling you about Edward, the founder of our outreach colonies, the person with the greatest experience of the early days of Green Declaration. He was part of the administration established to put everything right, with the Restoration Plan, and there was a hell of a lot to put right. He recognised how awful Man's destructive power had been and he also knew how conscientious everyone was to repair civilisation, to move things forward after the problems. He helped to create the wonderful upstanding principles upon which all was to be achieved. And then he witnessed the descent into greed and corruption that followed. He had little power over the High Council that was formed, based on covetousness and materialism for the powerful few. He just held on to those friends who had integrity and a belief in the common good and they formed the basis of the first covert outreach community."

"Mystica has a lot of knowledge about the corruption, the danger, but it is still somewhat locked away in her mind," said Marnie. " I think she will be in the forefront of any campaign to make the present administration conform to a proper democratic process."

Torrey and Juno sat back and said nothing for a moment.

"Unbelievable," said Juno.

"And yet," said Torrey, "totally credible. And I, for one, will want to play my part in whatever happens."

"That's my boy," said Joseph.

Chapter 27   Mystica and Benedict

"I'm not quite sure where things are with you at present," said Benedict. "Have you had any further flashes of memory?"

"Yes, I have had a horrible moment where I recall plunging into water and not really caring whether I survived or not. I can't call to mind what triggered it or if I was on my own or with others. It's hazy, but I remember forcing myself forward until the waves were covering me; and then having the most incredible feeling that I wanted to live. Just in case. But just in case what?"

"I'm glad that you decided on something a bit more positive than drowning. It's not good for you, you know!"

They laughed.

"I feel so happy to be here," said Mystica, "in spite of the bits of my mind that haven't quite sorted themselves out. Benedict, I can't tell you how much I feel I owe to you and the Baxters. I know that I feel especially close to you and Guy. I hope that's not too forward, but I can't waste time being too subtle these days."

"That's really rather inviing."

"I am hugely embarrassed now. I was never as brazen or even self-assured as that before. I can't believe what I said. Presumptuous, to say the least!"

"Mystica, your 'boldness' leaves me no alternative. I knew there was something special about you from the moment I set eyes on your rather bedraggled self and helped you back to the human race! I have had some hard years and have met nobody I have felt so close to, nobody I would rather be with, than you. That's pretty audacious for me and I wouldn't have said anything unless I felt that you felt something a bit more intimate than just friendly."

He turned to her, put his arms round her and gently kissed her.

"Was that alright?" he asked. "Not too much, too soon?"

"It was wonderful. I would like a repeat performance please."

She was suddenly lightheaded and trembling.

"What's wrong?"

"I don't know. Nothing and yet something. It has reminded me of a past feeling of love and I'm on the edge of remembering who and what. And I know that there was a baby involved. Not mine. I wasn't allowed to have a child. Oh Ben, I don't want anything to spoil this."

"I won't let it," he said, but there was an ominous feeling in his heart that the past was going to catch up with her in this new relationship.

At that point a rather beautiful teenage girl came over the dunes and caught up with them.

"Hi, you must be the wonderful mystery lady I've heard about."

"Susannah, this is Mystica. Mystica, this is Susannah Templeton, one of our young resident beauty queens in Seadrift."

"Oh Ben, I do love you! I've just been chatting up your good-looking son. He is not a patch on his old man of course. Don't you think Benedict is just the most handsome dreamboat you could imagine, Mystica? He stole my heart years ago."

"Must have been when you were about 4 and I was giving you your booster jab," said Ben.

Mystica smiled. She was quite unused to such flirtatious banter, although at the back of her mind there was the hint of a young girl in First City who was teasing and playful and whose actions she had misunderstood. But beyond that she couldn't remember.

"Hi Susannah. Nice to meet you."

"You staying with the Baxters still? I know Juno brought you back from the brink of death on the beach. Nothing so exciting has ever happened in Seadrift before. So romantic!"

"Well, Juno certainly rescued me and, yes, I am staying with her family at the moment. Not sure how exciting I found things, but I'm very happy to be here. And so well looked after."

Susannah cast a glance out of the corner of her eye towards Benedict.

"The Baxters are a hugely welcoming family and I was so lucky to be found by Juno and nursed back to health by the wonderful Marnie."

"Of course," said Susannah. "They are fantastic. Torrey is a bit of a dreamboat too, isn't he?"

Mystica laughed. "A bit out of my age range!"

"Mmm!" Susannah shot another quick look across at Benedict.

"Well, I wondered where you were." Guy came over the dunes and caught up with them. He was such a good-looking boy thought Mystica, and his ready smile made her feel like a welcome part of his family already. Things would be good she felt.

"Hello Guy, light of my life," said Susannah with a twinkle in her eye. "I'll swear you get more handsome every day!"

"Oh hi, Susannah. How're things with you?" Guy looked a bit embarrassed.

"All the better for seeing you (and your lovely Dad of course)," said Susannah.

Susannah was obviously a great girl for a cliché thought Mystica.

"So when are we going for one of those great, lonely hilltop walks, just the two of us?" asked Susannah and simpered at Guy, dropping her eyelids and peering through the lashes provocatively.

"Yeah, great idea," said Guy. "I'll, er, call you."

"If I don't call you first." Susannah laughed and skipped off shouting her goodbyes as she went.

"Bloody hell," said Guy. "What am I supposed to do with *that*?"

"By *that* I guess you mean Susannah?" asked Mystica with a broad grin on her face.

"Well, yes. She gets me all confused and I never really know what to say. It's not that I don't like her, but she frightens me I think!"

"I think Susannah is really quite unsure of herself and is trying to bolster her own confidence. I guess you could try and relax a bit and just treat her like a good friend, being careful perhaps not to be alone with her."

"But are all women like that? If so, I'm out of it! I don't have any experience of romantic relationships so I don't really know. But I can't think that's right. You're not like that!"

"Thanks Guy, I'll take that as a compliment. I was never given the opportunity to be flirtatious, living in the restricted areas of First City all my life, but I don't think it would ever have been my style."

Benedict smiled at her and squeezed her arm. "I think Mystica is right. Susannah is trying to boost her own confidence, but it's good to be given some advice as to how to deal with it. Like Mystica, I think Susannah will appreciate your friendship."

"I'm sure she really doesn't mean anything calculating by her actions - she's just a natural born flirt. But she will also mature and choose when it's appropriate to use her teasing and when it isn't. That time will come. She's obviously a fun person."

"Thanks Mystica. Exhausting, all that! I'm going on home." Without thinking he instinctively gave Mystica a quick kiss on the cheek and jogged off back to the Eastman unity.

"Thanks," said Ben. "You are just what he needs and he knows it. And, well I know it too."

Mystica was thoughtful for a while and they went on walking in a companionable silence until Ben said "Anything cropped up? Something remembered? Anything you want to talk about?"

"Philip."

Ben sighed. "I felt sure there would be someone."

"Philip and Louis."

Benedict waited.

"Philip and I found love for the first time in our lives. He had been partnered and they had a baby, Louis. They were friends but not much more and I remember the day he came to my door to ask if I would look after Louis. He had to go to the clinical quarter. His partner, Jo, had been involved in some awful accident. Of course 'accident' was somewhat inaccurate. She had asked too many questions about the death of her father, and was getting too close to the uncomfortable truth. So she had to go. Philip and I connected straight away. I'd never felt anything quite like it."

"So where is Philip now?"

"We stayed with Edward for a while and then he suggested we should journey on to an outlying colony. We set out and part of the way to wherever we were going Philip went back to collect something of mine that was precious to me. But he should never have gone. It was foolish of both of us to think that an object of sentimental value should be so important. It was too dangerous."

She outlined what had happened next, the arrival of Henny, the news that Philip had been taken into custody by Lucas and the sure knowledge that he would never return to her. As she told Benedict of those awful moments when Henny told her what had happened, she wept. The tears flowed freely and Benedict held her tightly and let her give full rein to the outpouring of grief that she felt. He understood her anguish only too well and it brought back memories of the misery and heartache he had experienced when Ellie was taken. He found his tears mingling with hers.

After a while she pulled back and dried his tears with her hands.

"It is liberating in some way to have been able to call this to mind, and now I know that my disappearance into the sea was of my own making, until I got under the waves. Then I could feel a determination, in spite of everything, not to give in. It wasn't an easy decision, but I have a grittiness in me that makes me change course if I think I have gone down the wrong road."

"Thank God for grittiness," said Benedict. "Mystica, I don't know what to say other than you have brought joy back into my life and Guy's too. I can imagine how hard it must have been up there in your mind to come to terms with this. Losing someone through the High Council is appalling. There's no way to deal with it through the compassion of friends because friendship isn't allowed. And, for you, alone in an unknown environment, it must have been terrifying. Perhaps, for us both, there is the opportunity to experience a second love. It can happen more than once you know."

"Ben, I think I already have a great tenderness for both you and Guy, and I am contented in a way I have never really been before. There were some moments with Philip, when we stayed with Edward, that were not perfect, but I loved him in spite of a blip or two."

"Do you feel you can move forward at some time and convert the tenderness to love?"

"I know I must let go of the past, and that's the first step I guess. I will never forget Philip, just as you will never forget Ellie, but I think that will only strengthen what we have. I feel almost liberated from my past in some way. It's so strange, but you have given me something I never had before, even with Philip. A kind of liberty and a great feeling of being cherished and cared for. I know I have the freedom to love."

"I love you Mystica, unlike any other love."

"I love you Benedict, and this love is unique."

Chapter 28   Philip and Lizzie

Philip thought a lot about Lizzie. She was a gentle girl and he wondered about her baby due in a few months. Will's child, but without a father. He knew just how important a father figure was in a child's life, if the father figure was the right person.

He felt that Lizzie had the capacity for love and compassion that was going to be much needed in the future. She was in that respect, in some ways, not unlike Mystica, although Mystica had been used to an independent life, self-governing and self-reliant in soul and body.

He wondered, not for the first time, how it could possibly be that she could have decided to take her own life. She was a determined person, not the kind of character to give up easily. But the evidence had been in front of him; her footsteps went one way and one way only.

He made his way into the nursery section to collect Louis and there, sitting on the floor with her back to the door, was Lizzie with Louis on her knee. His arms were around her neck and she was softly humming a tune to him while she rocked gently back and forth. He had obviously had a busy day and his eyes were drooping with sleep. Philip stood and watched. He felt a tenderness for this girl who was so drawn to his son. And he trusted Louis's instincts in selecting someone to love. He and Lizzie had so much in common in terms of loss, which led to a strong mutual understanding of grief and heartache. He didn't know how she might feel about him, but he already felt the stirrings of something stronger than affection. It was early days for them both, but he suspected there was little time to be lost.

Philip had realised that things were unsettled in First City and that times of change were ahead. This had been in Edward's mind when he wanted Mystica, Philip and Louis to travel to one of the outlying communities. He had hinted that there was an important role for them both within a new structure, but had suggested that they needed some time to get to know each other properly as a family first, away from the main community. They hadn't had the opportunity to experience this before events overtook them. Perhaps it wouldn't have worked out between them at all thought Philip.

He walked quietly over to where Lizzie was holding Louis and put a finger to his lips. She smiled and Louis opened his eyes and grinned at his father. Philip carefully took the sleepy boy from Lizzie. Louis immediately grizzled and held his arms out towards Lizzie. She stood up and took him back again.

"I'll carry him back to your unit if you like," she said. "He must like my perfume!"

Philip talked a little about Henny and Brooks, without divulging any secrets. He just said how much he appreciated Brooks' interest in Henny's artwork and how important it was for her to have this acknowledgment of her talent.

"He's an interesting man, is Brooks," he said.

"A puzzle," said Lizzie. "But there are obviously hidden depths to him."

"I guess we all have things we hide away, but his secret world is well concealed. He seems very warm towards Louis," said Philip, "and, of course, Louis is definitely very fond of him!"

"Louis has a great capacity for affection and is so completely non-judgemental. When you are as closed away as Brooks seems to be, that must be hugely important."

"None of us has the right to judge anybody else I guess. But it is easy to do and sometimes difficult to avoid. Mystica was good at that and I try to follow her example, but I am not her and, when it comes down to it, I suppose I do things differently. When I think about it, we didn't really know each other for very long."

"Will and I were also together for a short time really. Partnerships happened swiftly for convenience, as quick pairings were advantageous to the authorities, and we were just lucky to have fallen for each other in such a big way. I realise that I have to get over the loss and move on."

"I feel the same way."

They had arrived at Philip and Louis's living quarters. Lizzie carried Louis in and gently laid him down on his cot. She covered him with a throw, then stood back and smiled at Philip.

"He's a lovely boy," she said. "A great credit to you. I hope my baby will turn out as perfect as Louis."

"I don't know about perfect. He has his moments. Thank you for carrying him back, and thank you for being a new friend to us both."

"I think it is more for me to thank you. I arrived here all at sea, having felt such misery, and you and Louis have made the world of difference to me. I feel I can go forward into whatever the future may hold."

She smiled at Philip. Instinctively he moved closer to her, put his arms round her and kissed her on the cheek. She moved round so that they were closer and their lips met. It was a sweet, tender and loving kiss that held the promise of something to come.

Chapter 29   Samuel and Henny

Samuel had spent some time talking to Henny and asked her if she would be his companion on the journey to the outlying communities. She was excited by the prospect of something so different from the normal everyday life she led and thrilled that Samuel had asked her. She was flattered to think that, in spite of her indiscretions, he trusted her enough to want her to be alongside him. "Edward wants me to be his successor, which is daunting to say the least. I mean, how do you follow that? This journey is to make contact and begin the business of bringing together all the communities so that we can organise the banishment of the existing regime. We need to assemble a true and principled state that will mend the hideous mismanagement and cruelty of the present administration. You are my chosen 'partner' in the rejuvenation of the people. Is that too awful? Will you come with me?"

"I am overwhelmed but I promise I will learn how to be tactful. I would love to go with you! I promise I will think five times before I act. You can depend on me and I won't let you down."

"Henny, I know you won't. I have every confidence that we will make a good team. You have already learnt some valuable and difficult lessons about making assumptions and I also know that you have heard about Brooks. Your willingness to accept him and your kindness to him confirms what I have always seen in you. Finding out that he is your old man must have come as an almighty shock and the fact that you haven't talked about it does you credit, but you can now talk to me if you want to offload."

"It upset me first off and I really lashed out at Mum."

"Not too surprising I guess. It must have come as a bolt from the blue. Not something that you could have possibly imagined, or been in the least bit prepared for. And your mother would be the first to accept that."

"No, but kicking off as I did is something I need to control. I really hope I don't let you down Samuel. I know I've teased the life out of you always, but it's only because I am so ...well ...fond of you really."

She reddened in embarrassment.

"And I do want to be a significant help to you. I'm sure I will go on learning and I give you official permission, here and now, to give me a kick up the backside if I even remotely let you down." Samuel laughed.

"Both you and I have a lot to learn and I am frightened about the future! I just hope that neither you nor I need too many kicks in the rear end to keep us on the right path."

There was a tentative shuffling sound outside the door and Henny went to look in the passageway. Brooks stood there and put his hand out to touch her face.

"You're going away for a bit," he said. "I have a gift for you. Keep drawing and you can show me what you've done when you come back."

He passed across a book with blank pages and a set of watercolours. The book was made with paper that Brooks had made himself, and the paints were colours that he had created, vivid and beautiful.

"Wow, thank you so much!" said Henny. "The colours are gorgeous and the paper is beautiful. I hope I do them both credit. This is the nicest, most precious gift I could have been given." Instinctively she leant across and kissed him on the cheek.

"Be safe," he said, and then he was gone.

"Look!" she said to Samuel.

"I saw," he said.

The time came for them to leave. A couple of bags were packed, light enough for them to carry the first part of the journey until they reached the place where they could collect the vehicle that would take them the rest of the way. This was housed at a place called

Penvalley, one of the very small outlying units closest to the First City group that acted as a lookout post to be a first-line defence and add to the protection of all the communities. Food provisions for the journey would be supplied from here and anything else that was necessary. The all-purpose land cover vehicle was a self-charging silent machine, small and neat, that had a wraparound chameleon cover that could change colour according to where you were, should the need arise for concealment.

Henny hugged Ava and Edward. She then went up to Philip and Lizzie.

"Be happy," she said.

Out of the corner of her eye she spotted Brooks looking from the corner of the passageway. He raised one hand and she waved back to him, just before he scuttled off back to his workshop.

They made their way, silently and cautiously, out of the community and onto the deserted streets of First City, moving through the shadows until they were beyond the edge of the city and into the beginning of coarse and uneven territory. They still kept to the outer edges of the territory, keeping a close and watchful eye all around them. But this was not an area where the governing body of the High Council ever considered patrolling; they were sure that the population of First City were indoctrinated sufficiently to ensure that they never stepped out of line.

They arrived at Penvalley and the gatekeeper was waiting with the vehicle fully charged and ready to go.

"Hello Samuel, I'm Ross, keeper of the gate and provider of sandwiches and water! I think I've put in everything you might need," he said.

"Thanks Ross. This is Henny."

Henny smiled but kept silent.

"So, where are you going first?"

"Classified information," laughed Samuel. It would not be appropriate to talk about destinations with anybody and the gatekeeper should have known that.

"Sure, I understand. Apologies. I don't get to see much action here, so your trip is quite exciting for me too."

"We'll be back in a few days," said Samuel. "But I imagine there is no hurry to have this machine returned?"

"No, no rush at all. Anyway, we have some spares if needed."

"Thanks, Ross, and sorry I can't tell you anything more. It's an important mission though and I'm most grateful to you for your help. I'll try and stay a bit longer next time I come!"

"That would be good. I'm somewhat starved of good company! Go well."

Samuel made up his mind to ensure that he made friends with this man. It was important to keep somebody like him firmly on board. So much depended on people who seemed to have the most insignificant role, but without whom there was the strong probability of considerable danger lurking around every corner. He also decided to institute a rota system so that one man shouldn't have to always work in this monotonous situation for too long at a time.

They set off over the coarse terrain. Luckily the wheels made adjustments for the uneven ground and things were reasonable. After an hour the ground seemed to level out and they could see an expanse of dark woodland ahead.

"We'll just move into the first line of trees and stop here for a bite to eat," said Samuel. "Our way lies the other side of this wooded area and the tree line is quite thick. My automatic navigator tells me we are on course and we're actually due to arrive tomorrow."

"Arrive?"

"Yes. I'm sorry. You don't know where we're going, do you? I haven't told you much, have I?"

"Not a lot, but I'm OK to wait until you're ready."

"Well, I also know that you have learned about your brother, Torrey, just recently. We are going to that outlying community by land, the section where your brother lives with his family. It is called Seadrift and it's on the coast."

"What? I can't believe it! So, I will meet him. That's incredible."

"Henny, he has been told about his background, but only recently like you. I don't know how the family there feels about all this, so this will be a test for your diplomacy I guess."

It was starting to get dark when they stopped and parked in a small gap between the trees that enveloped them with their shadowy branches. Henny felt protected by both the trees and by Samuel. Travelling in the dark was a potential hazard for all sorts of reasons, so Samuel suggested they waited until it was light before they carried on. The vehicle had two thick blankets in the back and a couple of soft cushions. A heated unit in the vehicle provided some piping hot coffee and Samuel fell asleep as soon as he had finished his drink. Henny lay awake for a long while, listening to the night sounds and the murmur of the wind in the trees. She felt a mixture of excitement and contentment. Things were changing and she felt sure that life was never going to be the same again.

Chapter 30   Benedict, Samuel and Henny

The first light of dawn woke Henny and for a split second she felt completely disorientated. "Where the hell...?"
She turned and saw Samuel beginning to stir. She looked closely at his face, at the early morning stubble appearing on his chin, at the faint smile that was almost always there and watched as his eyelids started to flicker.

"What the hell...?" he said.

"Just what I was thinking," said Henny and laughed.

"Right, a quick breakfast and then we'll make a start," said Samuel.

Henny unpacked some bread and cheese and made some more coffee from the heated unit. She switched on an interior light and watched as Samuel gave his chin a cursory review with his shaver, getting rid of the worst of the stubble by feel.

"I could do with a shower," she said.

"Tricky. We'll have to rough it a bit for now," said Samuel. "I forgot to order the room with four-piece bathroom fittings this time. But I guess they'll have water where we're going."

Finishing breakfast and making time for a quick pee behind a tree was next on the agenda and then, as the sun's rays slowly started to push their way between the dense branches, there was enough light for them to make a start. The vehicle navigation took them through the densest part of the forest to the other side where the vegetation thinned out somewhat.

"Over to your right," said Samuel, "and beyond those hilly bits, about a mile distant, is the sea."

Henny was hugely excited.

"Are we anywhere near where Mystica came?" she asked.

"And tell me more about Seadrift, where we're going."

"You mention Mystica and that's where we are going. We will see Mystica."

"What do you mean?" Henny looked alarmed and suspicious at the same time. Was Samuel playing some awful teasing game with her? Not like him to be cruel, to play on her frailty, a part of her life she would rather forget.

"Henny, Mystica is alive and well. She didn't drown but was washed up on a beach at Seadrift. She was taken in, nursed back to health and cared for by the Baxter family - your twin brother is their son."

Henny gasped. "I can't believe it. That's such fantastic news. Best I've heard for ages! I can't wait to see her."

"We have to be careful. She had significant memory loss and it might not all have returned. I just don't know, so we have to be extra cautious, particularly regarding Philip and Louis."

"Oh God, yes! Philip and Louis. Philip and Lizzie in fact! Had you noticed?"

"Pretty obvious, I'd say, so there's another reason to tread softly. As far as I am aware, Mystica thinks that Philip was removed to be treated and I don't know if she has heard anything different. These communities tend to keep themselves fairly separate. News filters through only sporadically and, anyway, why should they know about Philip at Seadrift? It's only very recently that Edward got to hear that Mystica had been rescued and was being looked after in the community. Understandable really, as it was only very recently that she remembered about Edward and First City. So far, she doesn't seem to have remembered about Philip."

Their journey continued with the route becoming less rutted, the woodland giving way to grasslands and sand dunes with the strong salt air of the sea starting to hit their senses. They lapsed into silence, both aware of a mixture of excitement and apprehension. Samuel realised that this was the beginning of his time as Edward's chosen successor and he needed to ensure that he got things right. Henny was anxious about how Mystica was going to be able to accept the news concerning Philip. She also worried about their return to First City, in terms of how Philip would be able to deal with the news that Mystica was alive.

"One step at a time," said Samuel, more to himself than to Henny.

"Absolutely," said Henny. "One step at a time. My thoughts exactly."

They travelled down a gentle winding hill and, turning a bend at the bottom, there in front of them was the sea. This was the beach where Mystica had been washed ashore, her place of rescue, a place of sanctuary for her now. Samuel stopped the engine and they sat staring at the empty sands and the gentle rippling waves playing at the water's edge. There was such a sense of peace, unlike anything Henny could ever remember experiencing before, and the natural sunlight was fresh and new. The only sounds were the soft ticking of the vehicle cooling down and the screech of seabirds. Henny was enchanted. Samuel wondered what to do next.

From the far side of the beach Benedict saw them and came striding across. He had been expecting their arrival to be a little later and realised they had wasted no time in their travelling.
Samuel and Henny got out and stood on the sand for a second, marvelling in the grittiness which yielded to their footprints. Samuel walked towards Benedict and met him, his hand outstretched in greeting.

"Samuel! Hello, I'm Benedict. You made good time. You obviously didn't hang about once you got going! No problems on the journey?"

"Benedict, good to meet you. The journey was very smooth, except for the bumpy road! We stayed to sleep overnight in the forest and at first light we set off. I didn't want to waste any time. This is Henny, by the way."

"Wow, yes, Henny. Mmm. Hello Henny. I'd have recognised you anywhere!"

Henny felt suddenly rather shy and just managed to say "Hi" and smile at Benedict. It was hard to know quite what to say. Benedict obviously knew her brother.

"We've organised that you should come to my place to stay. The Baxters are pretty full up and there's only me and my son Guy at home so we have the space. I can take you over to meet the Baxters later perhaps, but you might be glad of a bite to eat, a wash and a rest first. You'll meet up again with Mystica as well. She's pretty much a celebrity round here. She's been through a lot but she's doing remarkably well and her memory has largely returned. She's going to be a great asset to the community here. We've all become very fond of her and I think that in the days to come, she will play a very important role in what lies ahead."

Samuel, as all leaders would want and need to do, had researched Benedict's background. He knew, from Edward, that Benedict had lost his life partner and that Ellie and Ben had achieved a love that had been denied to most partnering in First City. His medical training had meant that the authorities would be wary of him - he would be more likely to question and create problems for them than most people. Any form of disruption was something that always needed to be nipped in the bud, lest it spread like an infection. He was hastily taken in by Edward, with his son Guy, and they were sheltered and cared for before moving on to Seadrift and helping to establish one of the first outlying communities. Benedict was seen as the local unofficial leader of Seadrift and he was the point of contact between the First City community and the local group.

"So, Mystica is OK is she?" asked Henny. "No ill effects?"

"She's doing just fine," said Benedict. "She's made a huge difference to Guy and me. A wonderful girl."

Samuel and Henny looked at each other, both of them aware that further complications seemed to be developing.

Chapter 31   Torrey, Henny, Juno, Samuel, and others

Benedict guided Samuel and Henny to his unit and introduced them to Guy, who had been busy organising sleeping quarters for their guests. Guy shook hands with Samuel and then looked at Henny and his jaw dropped open.

"Hell's teeth," he said. "A clone, a replica! Well, almost." Benedict glared at him.

" God, I'm so sorry. That sounded rude. I didn't mean it to be. But, not the most tactful thing to say."

"Don't worry," said Henny with a huge grin on her face."It's what I do all the time. My mouth has always been a bit wayward. Samuel will confirm that."

"That's so true," said Samuel, " but you are learning. Henny, you'll be the soul of discretion by the time we get back to First City." Guy had also sorted out a late breakfast and the four of them sat down to eat. Various fruits and berries, plus some cereal and toast and freshly squeezed orange juice were on the menu. He did seem able to do breakfast then, thought Benedict.

Samuel still felt somewhat on edge. The enormity of his responsibilities dawned on him more and more each day, and the visit to Seadrift was just the start of establishing what lay ahead. He was worried about how things would be for Mystica and Philip, since both of them had come to terms with what seemed indisputable - the loss of each other - and had been determined to move on. Benedict showed them to their sleeping quarters - two small units with an interconnecting door. Samuel smiled. Early days he thought.
Benedict left them to unpack the few bits and pieces they had brought with them and Samuel mentioned his uncertainties about Philip and Mystica to Henny.

"I'm not quite sure how to deal with this," he said. "I'm sure you detected what Benedict obviously feels about Mystica. It's a love triangle plus one, or something."

"You know, I think you can leave that complication up to the four of them to sort out," said Henny. "Besides, we don't know how Mystica feels, do we? And you will have far bigger fish to fry."

"Henny, you're right. I think I'm just trying to put other, more complex things to the back of my mind. But you are right, they can sort their own problems out. I think I am feeling the weight of responsibility hanging rather heavily on my shoulders today."

"You'll be fine, Samuel. It's all a bit new at the moment and I think Benedict will be your first local leader by the looks of things. I get the feeling that Guy will be his assistant. He may have to learn a bit of tact along the way of course!"

Samuel roared with laughter.

"What?" asked Henny. "Oh, you mean me? I'm learning every day and my mouth is staying firmly shut when in doubt."

"I'm sorry, and I'm just teasing. I know you are learning fast. And what you said about Philip and Mystica makes sense."

"Well you can't deal with everybody's problems. And you do have some more important issues to wrestle with."

"And I know you will be a hugely important person to help me. You've already sorted one thing out for me in my mind and you are quite right. Philip and Mystica, plus Lizzie and Benedict, have to disentangle themselves. I must now use some time to talk to Benedict and establish a firm line of communication. I think he needs to come back to First City with us and we can make him our primary outlying area leader. I get a good feeling about him. I sense a man of integrity and good judgement."

Guy took Henny over to the Baxters' unit, leaving Samuel and Benedict to talk. When they arrived, Guy introduced her to the family and then left. As Henny suspected, Benedict wanted Guy to be his right hand man and needed him to be a party to discussions from the beginning.

Marnie came forward and gave Henny a big hug.

"Welcome Henny. It's good to meet you. This is my man, Joseph, and my two tearaways, Torrey and Juno. Mystica is no stranger, of course."

"This has to be about the most exciting time I've ever had," said Juno.

It was obvious to all straight away that Henny and Torrey were twins and Mystica remembered her first sight of Torrey which struck a chord somewhere in her deep down, although her mind was full of jumbled images at the time and she wasn't sure what she was recalling. Of course, it was Henny! Henny's eyes and a look of Ava about them both.

"Bloody hell," said Torrey, "it's almost like looking in a mirror."

"I guess we have a bit of catching up to do," said Henny. "My life has run on different lines to yours, but I still feel somehow that I have known you for ages."

"You must have some time together on your own," said Joseph.

"To fill in the gaps I guess."

"That would take forever," said Juno. "I would leave the gaps just as they are."

It was obvious that there was a lot of ground to cover and it wouldn't happen in an instant, but Henny looked across at Mystica, thinking of gaps and missing people, and felt a little shy. She didn't know how Mystica would acknowledge her and if she would understand, in some way, the manner in which Henny had blurted out the news about Philip and his abduction. She decided to just wait and see.

"Henny! How wonderful to see you," said Mystica and, like Marnie, she gave Mystica an enormous hug. "Marnie, do you mind if I steal Henny away and take her for a walk? We also have a bit of catching up to do."

"A good idea," said Marnie. "I daresay her brother can spare her for a while!"

"More gaps!" said Juno. "We'll 'catch up' later, Henny."

Mystica led the way down the path to the beach. The tide was coming in and the waves washed over the rock pools. Henny was fascinated by the little pools that were brimming over with life.

"I must come back tomorrow with my sketch pad and water colours," she said. "Brooks gave them to me as a parting gift."

"Oh yes, of course, Brooks," said Mystica. "A very special person with enormous talents and skills but shut away. I loved the way he started to bond with...with Louis, you know?"

Henny nodded. They went and sat on a rocky outcrop and watched the seabirds dipping into the waves to catch an early supper. Henny just loved the sounds of waves and wild birds, the scents of the sea and the beach-lined flowers, the warmth of the sun and the freshness of clean, clear air.

"And I think he connected with me to some degree. We had some good moments, and I felt he was a man of great sincerity underneath his obscurity. He wanted to be insignificant and he covered up his personality with an individuality that was eccentric," said Mystica. "But he was beginning to emerge to a few chosen people and I was fortunate enough to be one of them."

"I discovered, just before I came away, that Brooks is my father."

"Oh my stars!" said Mystica. "How extraordinary! So why, what...?"

Henny filled in the background, such as she knew it from Ava. Ava, the ever patient partner waiting in vain for Brooks to return to her, first of all in his mind.

"I was clumsy and unkind when I found out and I had to put things right with my Mum. I hadn't thought about her and how she had felt all these years. I only thought about me and how I seemed to have a loony for a Dad. I had no idea what to do or what to say to Brooks. I felt it was all too horrible. Better to have a father I didn't know and I could let my imagination run riot, invent him and see him any way I wanted. I'd never really thought about my father and who he could be, but Brooks would never have been on my list of possibles. I had a long talk with Edward and... and others, which helped and somehow

Brooks started to show an interest in my work which was wonderful. I really appreciated his input, although he used few words. I could just tell what he felt from his facial expressions and, from those limited words, it meant more to me than I could express."

"I'm so glad," said Mystica. "Things will come together for him now, I'm sure, and you are just what he needs. Fancy Brooks a father! And he has some wonderful genes to pass on. Your painting talents have come directly from him and must be treasured. And Torrey's artistic side too."

"I think we can develop a special relationship if I go very slowly about it. My lack of tact is something I'm working on and I made a special effort to befriend Brooks before Samuel and I came away."

"So, what about Ava?"

"Mum had a great feeling of sadness that Dad, Brooks, has yet to acknowledge her. I hope it will happen. I can't think of him as 'Dad' somehow."

"Brooks has some hidden depths and I'm sure that with gentleness and patience he will come round to re-establishing his partnership with Ava. I think I can understand that, of all relationships, losing that bond with Ava must have been the most damaging and he wouldn't want to risk that again."

Henny almost blurted out that Philip was alive and well, but realised it was not for her to tell Mystica. She had to leave it to Samuel to take the lead here and to decide how best to do it. She was somewhat proud of her ability to be tried and tested in the diplomacy stakes.

Down the beach at a run came Torrey, closely followed by Juno and Susannah Templeton.

"Aha! This is the lovely Susannah Templeton," said Mystica to Henny. "She has every boy in Seadrift surrounding her like the proverbial bees round a honeypot."

Susannah pretended a certain degree of modesty and shyness and Torrey and Juno laughed. Coyness wasn't part of Susannah's usual armoury. She noticed a particular warmth between Torrey and Henny, which she thought was strange on such a short acquaintance. She wasn't sure that she liked it.

"Anyone would think you'd known each other for years," she said.

She was Torrey's girl, as far as she was concerned. Nobody took the trouble to fill her in with the background, so she was left feeling suspicious and unsure, jealousy creeping in round the edges. Mystica noticed this and remembered what she had said to Guy about Susannah's lack of self-confidence that was hidden under a display of flirtatiousness.

"Well, it's often the way that you can make friends very quickly, almost instantaneously sometimes. I guess Torrey and Henny do feel they've known each other for years."

They all made their way back to the Baxters' unit and found Samuel was already there. There were introductions all round and Juno was especially attracted to Samuel. Samuel was very attentive towards her (as he was, she eventually discovered, to everyone - it was all part of his charm).

She took Henny on a bit of a guided tour of the unit and to her room.

"Samuel is just such a gorgeous bloke. Just my type. I can't believe that he's come to our unit and we've met him and he's due to take over at some time from Edward. I don't know Edward, of course, but it could be any time really, couldn't it?"

"Well, I don't know about that. Edward is incredible. He's old I know, but he's fit and strong and he's just always been there. Samuel is still in training, but yes he will take over from Edward when the time is right. Samuel is sensational, of course, and he will be as incredible, in time, as Edward, but he has a long way to go. He's totally dedicated, one hundred per cent, to the tasks that lie ahead of him and doesn't have much time for a social life!"

"Oh, I like to have a good time. All work and no play, you know?"

"At the moment "all work" is probably the order of the day for Samuel. Poor chap, but I expect he'll cope. But, hey, how about that fantastic Guy Eastman? Now there's an attractive man. He has a sort of dignity about him, and he's super good-looking."

"That's true, he is pretty special," said Juno. "Fanciable?"

"Oh definitely," said Henny.

Henny and Torrey spent an hour or so talking, playing music together and getting to know each other. It was a magical time and they were both absorbed by the extraordinary circumstances of their birth, first of all, and now their meeting.

Juno took Samuel for the same tour of the unit that she had that presented to Henny, although this was mainly on the outside and round onto the farming grasslands and underground winter gardens and conservatories. He was fascinated and could see that they had created a perfect place for growing and developing all kinds of farming. Juno said that her father was an expert in the cultivation of all kinds of crops and they had also built up some small animal husbandry, mainly chickens. The farming of animals was left to others in the community on the whole as was the development of some rather superior grapes for wine-making. Samuel was enormously impressed, and even more so when Juno said she was going to be carrying on the family business.

"I love the land" she said. "Don't mind getting my hands dirty and I just have to let the earth run through my fingers to know if it is good growing land, and what will suit it best."

"That's a gift," said Samuel. "I'm a real townie I'm afraid. I know nothing about the soil or growing food. I like eating it though."

"I guess Benedict and Guy are townies really, although we need them here to balance us! Guy made a huge impression on Henny didn't he? I think she's really quite taken with him. Don't blame her really. He's a lovely boy, bit old for me at the moment but you never know."

Was this Juno half-heartedly thinking that, if she might put a small cat among the pigeons here, it would turn Samuel towards her on the rebound?

Samuel was briefly unsure as to whether this picture of Henny having an interest in Guy was true or not. It would be a bit ridiculous after having met him less than 24 hours ago and common sense told him that this was improbable to say the least. However, he was taken aback to realise that this remote possibility had thrown him off balance.

Benedict and Guy joined them all for a meal later and Samuel watched interactions between Benedict and Mystica and between Guy and Henny, to get some clues to any sort of bond with both couples. He saw what was obviously a new warm friendship between Henny and Guy, which he would expect anyway. Between Mystica and Benedict there was the unmistakeable closeness of a couple developing a durable and indisputable love. This was interesting but he reminded himself that his responsibilities lay within the whole community, not in the romantic progress of two couples. He realised, however, that he needed to talk to Benedict about Philip and perhaps leave Ben to talk to Mystica.

Back at the Eastmans' unit, in the privacy of Samuel's bed quarter, Henny threw herself on his bed and let out a long sigh of contentment.

"What a day," she said. "What a great day and what great people! Such fun, and it was lovely connecting up with Mystica again."

In spite of what he had seen Samuel still felt disconcerted enough to confront Henny and determine her feelings about Guy.

"It was just something that Juno said. I guess it sounded a bit daft after one day to assume that you had suddenly fallen for him. But she was so sure that you thought he was 'fanciable', 'super good-looking' and 'pretty special'."

"What?" Henny laughed. "He's nice, but he could be a bit stuffy and boring I reckon. A bit too serious for me. I mean you're serious too, but different. No, I was just laying the trail for Juno to think about snaring him herself for the future."

"That all makes sense. I was just a bit uncomfortable I guess. I have to know that I can be totally sure of you if you are to be my life partner. This isn't just a working partnership for me. It's still early days and you're young, but I want to have children with you. Eventually."

Henny threw her arms round his neck.

"Does that mean that you love me?" she asked.

"Yes, I think I do," said Samuel and for the first time in their young lives they kissed. It was something that Henny had been waiting and hoping for over the years and she loved it. It was something that Samuel felt was an added responsibility and complication, but one he needed.

"Now," he said, disentangling himself. "We have to slow down on this. You do understand that, don't you?"

"Yes, yes of course I do, but I'm so happy."

He grinned at her and then said he was off to see Benedict. It was time to tell Benedict about Philip.

He found Benedict in his small study with Guy, and asked if he could have a few minutes alone with him. As soon as Guy had left, Samuel at once told Benedict that Philip was alive.

"Oh, God. I don't know what to say or how to feel," said Benedict.

"Am I right that you and Mystica have developed something special between you?" he asked.

"We both felt it was time to leave the sorrow and misery of the past and look to the future. Yes, we love each other and it is a love that has been supported by a mutual understanding of grief. A grief that we have come through and come to terms with. But how can this be? How can it be that we never heard?"

"I imagine nobody knew for some time that Mystica had survived, so why would the news about Philip filter through anywhere? Nobody knew where she was."

"God, what a mess! What a horrible, horrible mess."

"Philip wasn't taken by Lucas. He wasn't treated in any way. He just returned with Louis to the community thinking that Mystica had been taken by the sea. He still doesn't know that she is alive. I can tell Mystica myself, or you can. I think it best perhaps for the news to come from you. You and she have to do some thinking."

"This is just too awful. I can't believe that it is happening. I will have to tell her, of course, and I guess I risk losing yet another person I love, but I must tell Mystica and let her decide what to do."

"An added complication, or maybe not, is that Philip has met someone in the First City community and their love seems to be developing and deepening."

Benedict's heart quickened.

"Then there is a ray of hope perhaps."

"I guess all depends on how much Mystica really feels now for Philip and vice versa."

"I have come to realise that she is very much a person of sincerity and openness, with high principles. I would hate her to lose her wonderful sense of honour, but that might be at the expense of her returning to her love for Philip. I had such plans."

Samuel said nothing but touched him gently on the arm.

Chapter 32   Benedict and Mystica

Benedict took Mystica for a long walk across the dunes, along the beach and up onto the rocky hillside where the sea grasses blew and the gulls nested. They had said little on their walk, breathing in the clear air and feeling the occasional dampness of salt spray. They sat on the top of the hill looking out across the wide estuary and Mystica sighed with deep contentment.

"I just love it here so much, Ben. You have no idea. My life was somewhat complicated before and now, well now everything seems diamond. I finally have a destiny with you and Guy. Benedict, I can truthfully say I am so looking forward to a future with you, if you still feel the same way. I know that I love you and I am happy."
She looked out towards the sea, while she waited for him to respond. Benedict said nothing, but turned and looked away from her.

"Ben?" she said. "What is it? Have you changed your mind?"

He turned back and looked at her with tears in his eyes.

"Oh, my God," she said. "What's wrong? Is it something I've done?"

"I love you more than I can say. You have done nothing. It's fate. Bloody fate."

"What on earth do you mean?"

"I have to tell you straight out. I can't dress it up in any way that makes it easier for either you or me. It's Philip. Philip is alive and well and living back in First City."

Mystica looked at him in confusion.

"But that can't be. He was taken. Henny saw Lucas take him away. He was treated. I'm sure that was what happened and anyway if he was alive and well, why have I not heard about it?"

"Lucas had just met Philip and told him that he was trying to join the community to work on behalf of Edward and our group. Henny got the wrong end of the stick and came looking for you to fetch you back to First City, after leaving a message for Samuel. Philip meanwhile got safely back. Poor Henny found you and told you about Philip and Lucas. You both assumed the worst and she saw you run away through the trees. She ran after you, searching in the wrong direction, and she couldn't find where you had gone. Samuel and Philip came looking for you both and found Henny. She was distraught at having lost you. After some time they came to the beach and found your little bag of treasures and your footsteps going in one direction into the water. The conclusion was obvious; Philip was beside himself with grief and was persuaded, with some difficulty, to return to First City. I think it was only the thought of Louis that kept him from joining you in the sea. I am so sorry, my darling girl."

"But why did I not hear?"

"News of Philip didn't come through to Seadrift, as nobody knew that you had survived. And if they had known, where would you be? There was no way of knowing anything about you to begin with. So, news of your rescue and recovery never filtered through to First City, partly because your memory loss gave us no clues as to where you had come from. Bit by bit little pieces of information filtered through. It didn't occur to me to find out any more, however, when you told me that Philip had been taken for treatment. I thought that was a finality of some sort."

"What a mess. What a God awful mess, Benedict. I don't know what to think or do."

"I am so, so sorry. I love you and I need you, but I know that you must decide what happens next and I will support whatever you want to do."

"I don't want to do anything. I want to be here with you, sitting on the hillside watching the gulls and the tide coming in. That's what I want. But I can't have it. I can't have it any more!"

She suddenly fell apart and seemed to fragment with misery. Her body trembled and her chest shook as she dissolved into an outpouring of grief.

Benedict held her tightly and wept with her. Gradually her agonised crying subsided. She felt overwhelmed and exhausted, but knew she had to think about what to do next.

"Ben, I have to go back. I have to return to First City and meet Philip. I can't let things just slide. I need to be completely open or the future is lost."

"I know you do and, much as I hate the idea, this is the only course of action I would expect you to take. I can't bear the thought of losing you, but I will respect whatever you choose to do."

Benedict didn't muddy the water by telling Mystica that Philip appeared to have found another potential relationship. It hadn't appeared to be much more than a fragmentary piece of information from Samuel but, at the back of his mind, Ben held on to the hope that perhaps, just perhaps, things might work out.

They returned to the Eastman unit and, sitting round the table, Benedict said that he had told Mystica about Philip.

"God, it's certainly an unholy muddle," said Samuel. "I'm so sorry that we had to bring confusion to you. I don't know what else I can say."

"I still feel that I am to blame in a way," said Henny, her eyes filling with tears. "If I hadn't tried to find you to tell you what I had stupidly assumed had happened, things would be different."

"You're not to blame, Henny, any more than Philip or Lucas or anybody," said Mystica. "I am an adult. I should have stopped Philip from going back for a toy, just a stupid toy." She gulped and worked hard to keep the tears at bay.

"But Tiger meant so much to you, and Philip was so intent upon doing the romantic thing I suppose," said Henny. "It was part of his devotion to you."

Samuel stared hard at Henny and she stopped in her tracks. Any more reference to Philip's love was likely to cause more problems.

"I guess to take on board a new life in a new area everything needed to be just right," said Samuel, "and the cat in the snow globe was part of all that."

Benedict sat silently and Guy reached out to hug him. Benedict smiled thinly, appreciating the gesture of unconditional support from his son. He felt he couldn't look at Mystica. He so much wanted to feel indifferent to the whole situation but was utterly incapable. He had never had the ability to empower in the way that Ellie had; he was more a healer of bodies than souls. He was never more thankful when he saw that Guy possessed some of his mother's qualities already. Whatever happens, he thought, we'll survive.

"I admit I dread going back, but I know I must," said Mystica.

That evening Mystica did not return to the Baxters' unit. She and Benedict sat in the glow of some artificial firelight and they said very little but were aware of each other's feelings. They had developed a special perception that seemed to transcend words. Benedict knew the turmoil Mystica was undergoing; Mystica sensed how hard it was for Benedict to keep his counsel, to allow her to make her choice, which is what it amounted to. His silent support meant more to her than she could say and she instinctively reached out for him as they sat staring into the flames.

"Please can I sleep with you tonight?" she asked.

The following day, Benedict gently woke Mystica and said that he had arranged the vehicle for them. Samuel and Henny would stay at Seadrift and Guy would look after them. Benedict's discussions with Samuel meant that he needed to go to the First City community and talk to Edward. Samuel had asked him to be the main leading contact in the Seadrift community and he needed to discuss this with Edward. This would be the first part of the establishment of the new regime and the process would move, slowly at the beginning, until it had collected and established similar leaders in other outlying communities.

"I promise that I will leave you completely alone to be with Philip and make your own decisions, though I will find that incredibly hard. I do want to say, however, that last night was magical."

"I so wish things were different," said Mystica, "and I don't know what I shall do, but it will have to be the right thing, whatever that is, I suppose." She kissed him. "Last night was exquisite and I will always hold that memory in my heart."

Benedict smiled at her.

"I want, and need, to see Edward to talk about the future of the communities. Part of my job will be to ensure that there will be sufficient proper medical and social care and, in terms of the new regime, that will be one of my first priorities."

Chapter 33   Edward, Mystica and Benedict

Their journey took over two days. They took things slowly and carefully, stopping along the way to eat what they could manage of the slender rations they had packed and to make gentle love beneath the stars. It was a bittersweet time.

They left the vehicle at Penvalley. Ross, the gate-keeper, was pleased to see them, and may well have known at least some of the reasons for their journey, but he asked no questions.

They travelled the rest of the way on foot. Arriving at the First City community they were astonished to see Brooks waiting in the shadows with a variation on Samuel's red handkerchief sticking out of his pocket. This one was blue.

"Now that's about five steps forward for him. Apart from just being here, there's that handkerchief. But at least it's blue. He absolutely hates red!" said Mystica.

"Brooks, how good to see you," said Mystica and she instinctively leant forward to give him a hug. There was a momentary automatic recoil from Brooks but then he relaxed and smiled at her. She hoped she hadn't gone too far.

"This is Benedict."

Brooks nodded and Benedict came forward, his hand outstretched. Brooks tentatively shook his hand and then led them down the shadowy alleyways and passages into the secret entrance to the community. He took them straight to Edward's special garden and Edward was there waiting for them.

Edward enveloped them both in an enormous hug with a strength that belied his years. But he looked different somehow, thought Mystica. She realised that she had forgotten just how old he was, how craggy his features, how tired his body and yet how his eyes still held that wonderful shimmering warmth.

The tranquillity of his garden, with the gentle ever-changing rainbow colours, softly playing against the walls, relaxed them both, belying the turbulence that each was feeling deep inside.

"Oh, my dears, welcome both of you! Welcome! It's so good to see you, and Mystica I can't tell you how much I have rejoiced, with the rest of the community, to hear that you were safe and well! And Benedict, it's been too long."

"Edward, you haven't changed a bit," said Benedict.

Edward laughed.

"I suppose I should be concerned now about your powers of diagnosis on observing a patient, but I shall, instead, just take it as a giant compliment. Thank you, my boy! You, on the other hand, look relaxed and contented in a way that is quite different to how you were when you left us to go to Seadrift."

Benedict smiled. He couldn't speak but just looked at Mystica and then back to Edward.

"Ah! Yes of course. There may be some complications to untangle here, I imagine. Philip knows you are here, Mystica, and he has gone to the small recreation room. Henny is in the middle of rejuvenating it with a splendid new mural, to be completed on her return. I'm sure you'll be pleased. Nobody else goes there at the moment, since it is in the stages of redecoration so you can be on your own. I think you should go there and break the ice. There is quite a bit of catching up to do and some hurdles to be jumped. I hope they don't prove to be more like mountains, but I am sure you will come to the right decision."

"I know it won't be easy," said Mystica, "but I had no idea when we were travelling here just how hard this moment was likely to be."

A small table was prepared with some light refreshment, cold chicken and salad, fresh raspberries and a pitcher of freshly squeezed orange juice.

"Sit now. You've had a quite a journey with a lot to think about, but now have something to eat before you step off into the future, both of you."

"I'm not sure I could eat a thing," said Mystica.

"But you will try, won't you?" said Edward.

Mystica nodded.

"I suspect Philip may be as nervous as you are, but you certainly both have a lot to discuss. Meanwhile Benedict and I also need time to talk. Samuel has kept me up to the mark with how things are at Seadrift and I am delighted that Henny and Torrey have 'collided' with each other - I can't think of another appropriate word to use for either of them, although I haven't seen Torrey since he was very little."

"Torrey is, like Henny, very artistic. His talents lie in music more than visual arts, but he has a wide appreciation for someone so young and with so little exposure to the creativity of others," said Mystica. "The whole family have such a lot to offer to Seadrift as an emerging second community. They have obviously come a long way since the early days."

"That's due, in large part, to Benedict here and I understand, Ben, that your son Guy is likely to be a first rate assistant to you in leading Seadrift's governance."

"He will be. He's so like Ellie that he complements me. He can look at the deeper parts of the human character and get to the heart of things. I think he will make a wonderful counsellor to the community. There will be stressful moments, I am sure, and he will be a balancer for us all."

"I think you have the makings of a fine team," said Edward, "and others within Seadrift will be of huge importance in the basic and fundamental processes of moving forward towards the ultimate goal of restoring humanity to our people. You will need to produce a small team of individuals, who have their own special skills, to make a local administration. The system in each community needs to have, and retain, its own autonomy to a degree. Your success has always relied on your self-sufficiency."

"We have certainly produced a tight ship," said Benedict, "and that has been largely due to our self-government. Certainly, any small transgressions have been effectively dealt with through goodwill. We have had few problems to deal with at any time really."

"There will be more in the future I imagine," said Edward. "The larger an organisation grows, the harder it is to keep a tight rein on emerging difficulties, while retaining benevolence. The High Council's route was well-defined to begin with. Much needed changing after the events, and the Green Declaration was efficient but short-sighted - things got distorted and corruption took over. Many people will be more than ready to accept that a better way should be found, and compassion will be needed towards those you can take on board from among the misguided ones who mistakenly embraced the authority's principles. It will have been hard for them to do anything other than go along with the regime - fear makes us all weak and talking about one's deficiencies is hard. Guy's gifts will be more than useful with so many of these people I think."

"I can see it will not be an easy task," said Benedict.

"Meanwhile, Mystica, I think you should go and see Philip now. Benedict, you and I need to talk about how best you can support Samuel in what will be, for him, an enormous commission. I shall only be here for a small part of his journey, but enough I hope to be able to guide him a little."

"I'll go now. See you later," said Mystica, more to Benedict than Edward perhaps.

Chapter 34   Mystica and Philip

Edward and Benedict talked about the future for Seadrift and the other outlying communities. Edward suggested that perhaps Benedict and Samuel should visit some of these together. He said he thought that Benedict should provide a point of liaison among the outlying groups. He added that, although Samuel would be the overall guide through the difficult times ahead, he would be relying heavily on the help of Benedict and similar leading contact people from the other communities. There should be regular meetings and regular visits to each other's areas, something that had not really been done in the past; each commune had been almost entirely self-directed, and only when some specialist help was needed, as in Benedict's medical skills, was some contact made. However, Benedict had kept in touch via the general community web system, old-fashioned though it was. He had always felt the necessity to keep connections open.

"That's good," said Edward. "I felt sure you would have done. I'm afraid old age made me take my eye off the ball somewhat. It is essential now that associations are recaptured and all links are maintained. I will, of course, help as much as I am able, but my strength is waning."

"You look as strong now as I remember you on the day I left First City," protested Benedict.

Edward laughed.

"Either you are attempting to flatter me, or your observation skills as a doctor have taken a nosedive!"

"Well, maybe a bit older I guess. The skin has stretched somewhat."

"But the memory hasn't," said Edward. "That has most definitely shrunk. I still have some experience to offer, however, and I will as long as I am able. You won't be left on your own. Samuel has already undergone some extensive training and he can pass on what he has learned, as well as his own original ideas, which are innovative and worthwhile. On the other hand, he is still a young man and he will need the help and the wisdom that you have acquired over the years, plus your steadying hand. He doesn't rush into things and I know he will very much welcome your judgement."

"I think Mystica could offer a great deal of stability. I know she is committed to helping where she can."

Benedict looked a bit awkward mentioning her name.

"Quite right, Ben, and I had earmarked her for a leading role in the redevelopment of the system. I'm sure that will be more than possible but tell me, if you can, how things stand between the two of you."

"We have developed a closeness. I see it growing into an enduring love, and I know that Mystica feels the same. The existence of Philip provides a complication. I have to allow Mystica to make whatever decision seems right, but I hate it."

"I can see that this could be a problem, but Philip has grown close to Lizzie, one of our newer members. Let's just say I see it as something that the four of you will work out between you. Have patience."

Mystica met Brooks on her way to the small recreation room.

"I'll walk a while with you," he said.

"Julian, can I call you Julian?" Brooks nodded. "That would be lovely. I've missed you, but it was wonderful to see Henny a few days back when she and Samuel arrived at Seadrift. She's a very special girl. These murals everywhere are just wonderful. You must be proud of her."

Brooks looked surprised for a moment, his face questioning. But he knew about Henny and she was aware that he knew.

"Yes," he said. "Very special. My girl."

"She and Samuel make a good team and they will be back to help establish the new order. Your skills will be invaluable and they will so much want to include you in the design of the future."

"I have things to sort out first," he said.

"I'm sure you do and you will, but we are talking in the longer term, when your life has got onto an even keel again."

"Will you come back to First City?" asked Brooks.

"I...I don't know yet. I'm unsure where the path will lead me, but I will always make time to see you and to talk. I want to help wherever it is needed and it may be that Seadrift is my home. I don't know. You are having to face major decisions in your life too, so I know you will understand."

"Ava..." started Brooks.

At that moment the door to the small recreation room opened and Philip stood there. Brooks quietly disappeared from sight.

"Philip."

"Mystica."

They hugged and Philip led her into the room. He seemed awkward in his movements, as if he was unsure of how to approach this unexpected and peculiar meeting.

"Brooks and I were marvelling at Henny's work on the murals and talking about Henny's creativity. Is this her work in here?" She looked round at the unfinished art work on the walls, the scenes of coastal waters, a beach, seabirds and was amazed at the imagination shown by a girl who had never see the sea before.

"This is extraordinary," she said. "It's wonderful, so like Seadrift..."

She stopped, feeling awkward.

"So, what happened?" asked Philip. "You survived. You were rescued."

"Yes, I decided that abandoning life, when I thought you had been taken, was somehow spiritless. I was desperate, but so unsure of what I should do. I remember wading into the water and wanting to be swallowed up, to be consumed so that I didn't have to think any more. But then..."

"Then you changed your mind."

"I tried to think what you might have wanted me to do, and I tried to think back to what my grandparents would have expected me to do. I knew I had to try and survive, to give life one more chance."

"If I had only known. I have never felt despair like it."

"I think we both had the same feelings of grief and loss. But when I was helped back to recovery, I had little idea what had happened. There was just a large aching emptiness where my memory had been . I was looked after with extraordinary care, and bit by bit things returned."

"Then why didn't you try to get in touch?" asked Philip. "It was only the essential need to look after Louis that kept me going. I could, so easily, have followed you into the water if it hadn't been for Samuel reminding me that I had a son, a son who made me indispensable."

"When I remembered about First City, there was little point in getting in touch. Although I remembered First City, you and Louis had been blanked out of my memory. You were both just part of a tremendous loss that I couldn't name; it was like a bereavement. And then, when I did remember you, as far as I was aware, you were no longer there. You'd been taken."

"But I wasn't."

"And, of course, you assumed I had drowned, so I suppose there was no purpose to be gained in trying to find out if I had survived. And if I had, how would you ever find out where I was?"

"I should have done. I know that now."

"And I know I should not have taken Henny's assumption to be fact."

"I felt almost consumed with guilt that I had left you."

"And so was I. I was ashamed of the fact that I had allowed you to return to get Tiger, my 'cat in a snow dome'. How could I have been so stupid, so childish as to see it as important?"

"I was acting like a lovesick boy, wanting everything to be just right from the very beginning, and that included having the things you cherished so much around you."

"Perhaps we were both stupid."

"Acting irresponsibly certainly. And Henny will never really forgive herself for what she saw as her fault in all this."

"Poor Henny," said Mystica. "I guess that was one of the hardest lessons she has ever had to learn. How not to jump to conclusions. How to ensure that you can confirm things before you tell everyone that something is an actuality. I think she is, however, learning fast and, with Samuel to help her, she will be fine."

"I think we have to accept that no one is to blame. Circumstances were against us and maybe things for us were just not meant to be."

"I feel very confused," said Mystica. "So much has happened in such a short space of time and my mind has been in turmoil one way and another."

"I know what you mean but, for Louis's sake as much as mine, I had to make up my mind that life had to go on, I had to move forward. And I think I have. But I feel I need to talk things over with Edward and get the benefit of his advice over what I should be thinking, how I should continue."

"I have already got some time booked to talk to Edward. I need his guidance to clear my head and think about the future in all sorts of ways. He is the wisest man I know and he is so straightforward. Everything he says appears to disentangle the worst knots."

"We are children, aren't we? Needing 'parental' direction still. With Edward as the father figure."

Chapter 35   Mystica, Philip and Edward

Mystica approached Edward with something of a heavy heart. She had no idea what he was likely to say about how things had turned out for her and Benedict.

And she was bewildered by what she felt, or perhaps didn't feel any more, for Philip. She was unsure of his feelings too. He seemed in some way to have trodden a new pathway and she had no idea what that was about.

"I think I know what you are about to tell me," Edward said gently. "Benedict was quite right to leave you on your own to talk to Philip, but he made little secret of what you mean to him when we spoke. He says he feels sure that what he gives to you, you give back to him in return. Is that so?"

"Yes, it is. At first I thought I was just grateful to him for helping me to recover, but it was so much more than that and certainly I know that I want to be with him all the time. I want to hold him, to touch him, to be caressed by his breath. I thought I felt that with Philip and I think I did, but to a lesser degree. I had never had the experience of loving outside my family before, and it was new and exciting. I felt we were twin souls."

"And so you were," said Edward. "Twin souls in adversity."

"But I loved him so much. I think I still love him..."

"It is possible to love more than once and more than one. Love arrives in different ways, at different times, for different reasons. But the atmosphere is charged when a love is deep and ceaseless. And now tell me, what about Seadrift?"

"It's where I think I should always have been. I can sense everything about it that I believe is part of what I am. I love the sea, the air, the rocks, the waves, the cliffs, the grasses, the dunes, the birdlife, the sounds, the sun and the people. Just everything about it. I was so lucky to meet the Baxters, as well as Ben and his son. It's a small community and I was hoping to get to know them all, bit by bit."

"Fate sometimes takes a hand and plays an extraordinary part in shaping what's to come."

"I can't imagine returning to First City, or anywhere else for that matter, and being as truly and deeply fulfilled as how I feel at Seadrift. That is so selfish of me, I know. Hardly what you had in mind for me originally. I'm putting myself first and the establishment of a new regime second."

"That's perfectly in order. It is important that those who have a role to play in guiding the future need stability and contentment in their lives, in order to be truly supportive of others. If you spent part of your life feeling unfulfilled and miserable, the chances are that you would be less helpful to others. No, your happiness is paramount."

"I don't feel I altogether deserve happiness, and I keep thinking that what I have found is going to all dissolve and disappear, and leave me stranded and about to drown again."

"Well, it might, but we always have to take one day at a time and be grateful for all the good things. The time may come when life isn't so easy or clear cut. It's a risk we have to take. But now you have returned, and some decisions need to be made between you and Philip."

"I don't know what he feels at all. I think he may be as unsure about us as a couple as I am, but I want to be fair. We seemed so sure when we were here and in the early days in the apartment block in the city."

"A lot has happened for both of you in a relatively short space of time. All I would say is you must both be as honest as possible, at the expense of being hurtful if need be. You mustn't ever be part of a resentful relationship. That will only lead to more bitterness and *'what might have been'* feelings. Utterly no good to anyone and potentially destructive."

Edward sighed and yawned.

"You're tired and I must go," said Mystica. "I hope I haven't burdened you with all this too much."

"I need a short nap, my dear. That's all. And, as for burdening me, tush! I am so delighted to see you and I hope that some of what I have said will help you to come to a decision. I know it'll be the right one. I'm going to have a fifteen minute shut-eye and then I'm due to meet Philip. I'm sure he will be just as concerned as you are. By the way, have either you or Philip mentioned that word, '*love*', when you were talking?"

"No, no it didn't get a look-in," said Mystica.

"Could be a bit of a pointer," said Edward.

Mystica left and went to look for Brooks. He was in his workshop, busy with a complicated repair job, full of intricate little moving parts that actually weren't moving much.

"Can't stop," he said. "You alright?"

"Yes, I guess so," said Mystica. "Don't worry about me. You carry on. I haven't come to talk really, but you were the one person I could think of who wouldn't put any pressure on me, wouldn't ask any awkward questions and wouldn't pass judgment. Is it OK if I just stay and watch? My mind's too full at the moment trying to work out what I should do. I won't make a sound."

Brooks nodded and smiled.

Half an hour later Philip went to see Edward.

"So, how can I help you?" asked Edward.

"I guess I just need some of your wisdom to help me along the way," said Philip. "It was an almighty shock finding out that Mystica was alive. I was in the depths of misery when I came back here with Samuel and Henny and, if it hadn't been for them reminding me of my responsibilities with Louis, for two pins I would have rushed into the sea to be with her. It's crazy."

"Do you feel resentful that she decided to survive?" asked Edward. "Because, it must have depended at least a bit on her own will-power that she stayed alive."

"Resentful? God that sounds awful," said Philip. "Resentful? No, not resentful, but betrayed in some way. I don't mean it was any kind of deception on her part. It was as if life had played another trick on me. I had to come to terms with the fact that I wasn't going to have her in my life any more. That meant that I had to make a conscious decision to do the *'life goes on'* thing for both me and Louis."

"And so...?"

"Well, you know Lizzie. She and I found ourselves in the nursery quarter one day and I discovered a sympathetic listener. She already knew about Mystica and she was compassionate. She's a thoughtful, caring person who has been through her own hell and understood exactly what I had been through. I found myself making comparisons between Lizzie and Mystica and, to a certain extent, they have similar characteristics. I have developed strong feelings for her and I know that she feels the same way. Neither of us has made much of a move, however, with the situation being a bit awkward. Although deep inside I feel huge swathes of guilt about Mystica, I know I would like to support Lizzie, particularly as she has a baby on the way. But, I can't tell how Mystica will react and I don't want to hurt her. I somehow don't see her as the person she was. We had something really special between us and that has to be recognised."

"It came, for you, at a time of great stress and, for Mystica, when she thought she had an empty life. I think things are different now for you both. When you met earlier, did the word *'love'* enter any of your conversation?"

"No, but I'll always be grateful for the wonderful times we spent together."

"Not quite the same, is it?" said Edward, accepting that neither Philip nor Mystica had been able to use the word *'love'* to each other. "I certainly can't tell you what to do, except to say that both you and Mystica need to acknowledge openly how things have changed. Believe me, they have changed massively for Mystica too, and she has found contentment. Benedict, from Seadrift, helped Mystica enormously in her recovery and I'm not giving any secrets away when I say that I believe their friendship has developed into something that I believe will be sustainable in the long term. The next step is for both of you to appreciate that important leadership roles exist for you in the future that lies ahead and that other considerations have to be taken in the light of that. But first, talk together, all of you. You all have to be able to step forward into the future with sincerity."

Chapter 36   Mystica, Benedict, Brooks, Philip and Lizzie

Philip left Edward's quarters and went towards the small recreation room. He felt happier knowing that, for Mystica, there was something beyond the relationship they had enjoyed. On the way he met Benedict who was looking at the murals along the corridor.

"These are just wonderful," he said. "I hadn't realised just how talented Henny is."

Philip pointed down to the lower right hand corner of the wall. There, nestling in the undergrowth, half hidden among the bushes, was a small ginger cat.

"Good grief," said Benedict. "That's Tiger I guess?"

"Yes, and sometimes I think he's there to haunt me, to remind me that I was stupid enough to try and return to collect the snow globe. If I had been sensible I would have argued the toss and told Mystica that we could collect the globe on our next journey to First City. I guess I thought we probably wouldn't ever come back and, fired with a gallant and idealistic notion, I did the stupidest thing I could have done, and I left her on her own."

Benedict nodded but said nothing. If Philip had hoped for some kind of sympathetic response he was to be disappointed.

"It was stupid and, whatever happens in the future, I will always regret leaving her there. I don't feel guilt as such any more, particularly not now I know that she survived, but I will always recognise what a dim-witted action it was."

Again Benedict just nodded. Philip realised he couldn't extract any support from Benedict and changed tack.

"Come and look at this," he said and led Benedict into the recreation room. "This is the work of someone who has never seen the sea. What do you think?"

"She is certainly a girl with the most extraordinary imagination and skill," said Benedict. "I think she will be the perfect partner for Samuel. She will balance his rather more serious side with her spontaneity. Her search for diplomacy will always have to continue, I imagine, but she is learning and Samuel will always be an excellent teacher."

"Yes, she has always been rather quick to assume things and pass her thoughts on. They sometimes grew in their intensity as well, so the impact became all the more powerful. I could never blame her, however, for what happened to Mystica. I could never see the whole thing as anything other than my fault for a long time. Edward set me straight on that and made me see that blame couldn't be laid at any one person's door."

"From what I can tell, I think Mystica feels a large degree of responsibility for what happened. And circumstances have a way of setting things straight. Relationships are never one hundred per cent understandable or necessarily easy and the inexplicable happens all too often."

"I guess you know about loss only too well," said Philip. "I'm so sorry that your partner was taken. And you, like me, were left with a child to care for."

"It was hard and I could understand, only too well, Mystica's initial feeling that, thinking you had been taken, she just wanted to die. That's how I felt when I lost Ellie."

"Yes, when Jo died, it was a really hard time in my life. But, unlike you, we were not partnered in love, just partnered. We got along well, but there was no particular spark. It wasn't until Mystica came along and I thought I had lost her, that I wanted to wade into the sea after her. The thought of Louis and his needs were the only things that stopped me I think."

"I can see that. Mystica is an extraordinarily special person and I can't imagine losing her."

They were both quiet for a moment.

"I have made a new bond just recently and I feel strongly connected to Lizzie. She lost her partner, a love match like yours, and I feel we connect really well. She has a child on the way and I want to support her in being a parent."

"Can I meet your son?"

"I am always ready to introduce him to anyone in the world - well, in our world anyway - so yes, of course."

Brooks had a tea break coming up.

"Would you like something to drink?" he asked.

Mystica sipped her tea from a scalding hot brew. It was tinged with a sharp orange flavour and was delicious.

"You know, Henny is a truly remarkable young lady," said Mystica. "You obviously know that she has been partnered, in Edward's way, with Samuel and they have been companions for some considerable time. I think they know each other's idiosyncrasies and where there are faults, they will correct each other."

"I hope so. Samuel's a good person."

"And so is Henny. She is so talented and is so proud of you and the thought that she has inherited some of your skills fills her with pride. She's not afraid to bite the bullet as they used to say, but Samuel will teach her when it is appropriate and when it is better to sit back and wait."

"She's my girl," said Brooks. "My girl."

"And she has your talent," said Mystica. "You will have heard that she has met up with Torrey, her brother. A wonderful time for them both and I hope that Torrey will come back to First City and connect up with you and..."

Brooks quickly passed over a plate of shortbread biscuits he had made, as if to curtail the direction of that conversation. Mystica bit into one.

"Mmm!" she said. "Delicious. You have excellent culinary skills as well."

"I had a good teacher," he said.

"Julian, Henny and Torrey also have a wonderful mother. You know that, don't you?"

Brooks looked down at the ground and said nothing. Then, when at last he looked up, Mystica could see tears in his eyes.

"Fear and pain were strong company for me. They made me deny what I loved."

"You are one of the most wonderful people I know and I think everyone who knows anything about you feels the same. Edward is a champion of yours, you know."

"A busy man. Lots to do."

"Yes, but he never forgets how much he and the community owe to you, and he is always full of admiration for what you have achieved."

"I'm seen as an oddity by most people."

"You are unique. An individual and, like many people with imagination and creativity, there is sometimes an element of misunderstanding. That doesn't mean that people do not appreciate your extraordinary gifts and the wonderful skills you bring to the community."

Brooks listened to her with appreciation. Her understanding of him as a person had helped to raise his self-esteem.

"You know, Ava has never stopped loving you. She's never stopped hoping and waiting for you to return to her. Love is a strange thing. When you think it will never come to you, it does and it arrives with such strength. I love Philip and Louis still, but my new love for Benedict is greater than anything I can ever remember. Philip has found a new relationship with Lizzie and my destiny, I am sure, lies with Benedict."

"I remember Benedict from the time when Ellie was removed. He deserves some great happiness and I think you will give that to him in large amounts."

"I think it's time I went to see Louis," said Mystica.

Brooks walked with her as far as the cleaning unit where he went in to see Ava. In the doorway, Mystica hugged him.

"Be brave," she said. "Embrace your love."

On the way to the nursery she went into the small recreation room again and saw the marvellous murals painted by Henny. Again, she was overcome by the sheer brilliance of imagination shown by this girl who had never before seen the coastline, the waves, the sand and the rock pools that she had sketched in and partly painted. Looking at the walls she was surer than ever that this was the backdrop for her future, this coastal scene was the pathway for her with the opportunity for happiness with Benedict and Guy.

There were footsteps and voices outside the door and Benedict, Lizzie and Philip came in. Before Mystica could say anything, Lizzie came up and embraced her.

"I'm so glad to meet you, Mystica, and so glad that things have turned out so positively for you. Philip has told me all about you and the help you gave to him and to Louis, and the changes you had to make in your lives."

"And Benedict has told me how much you mean to each other," said Philip.

Benedict spread his hands out in a gesture that looked as if he just hadn't been able to help it.

"Well, Edward did say to be open and transparent and say things as they really are," said Mystica. "But I was expecting it all to be a bit more complicated. I thought I would have to explain things and make excuses for being fickle."

"What we had," said Philip, "was what we both needed at the time and it was love. I'm sorry, Benedict and Lizzie, but I have to tell you that I will never stop loving Mystica, although I want to make my lasting bond with Lizzie."

Mystica gave Philip a hug and whispered in his ear "And I will always love you."

At that point, Evelyn came in with Louis who rushed over to Lizzie for a hug.

Evelyn said "Louis has just pointed out that little figure of a ginger cat in the corridor mural. He was delighted to see it! Henny will be pleased."

"Louis, oh Louis how lovely to see you and how you've grown!" said Mystica. Louis looked at her, not quite able to remember who she was. She thought with a wry smile that maybe her ginger cat was more memorable than she was.

Mystica felt rather sad and somewhat discarded, although Louis grinned at her. It was apparent that he had eyes only for Lizzie as his mother figure. This was a decider for Mystica and she hugged both Philip and Lizzie. Louis joined in with what he saw as an exciting fun group embrace and Mystica remembered, so well, the lovely baby smell she found so enticing before. She sighed with disappointment at lost chances.

Benedict came over quickly and enfolded her in his arms. "We'll see," he says. "We'll see."

Chapter 37   Seadrift again

Benedict and Mystica spent some more time within the community, time for Benedict to talk to Edward and get a grasp on what difficulties would lie ahead and the ways in which he would be able help Samuel with the outlying units. It was obvious that from now on, communication was key and transparency the order of the day.

Mystica got to know Lizzie better and the more they were together the more she realised that Lizzie and Philip were tailor-made for each other. She had a strong sense of things being right for them, and it was a joy to talk to Philip about his growing love for Lizzie, without a hint of embarrassment or awkwardness. They both recognised that the fourteen year age gap between them, although it had appeared to mean nothing at the time, pinpointed the fact that in terms of maturity, Mystica had the edge. She and Benedict were of an age, and from that standpoint alone, her relationship with him was effortless. She was able to see things with great clarity; they had an immediate and often unspoken understanding. The path was even and smooth.

As the time approached for Benedict and Mystica to make the journey back to Seadrift they, with Philip and Lizzie, asked Edward for his blessing. He was delighted with how things had turned out, but counselled them all on keeping vigilant at all times, approaching the future with joy and expectation, but also with caution. He said he would like to make a trip to Seadrift, the furthest colony from home at present. Philip and Lizzie said they and Louis would travel with him as soon as possible. They looked forward to meeting the residents, and Guy in particular.

The morning came and it was time to say goodbye.

"You will always have a large part of my heart with you," said Edward to Mystica. "Be happy, but never forget the trials and tribulations of your early days in First City. Forgetting is the first step towards complacency."

"I am so happy," said Mystica. "But I know how easily things could come crashing down on us. I know that we're not all the same and some people will, I am sure, want to take advantage of a renewed system that seems to them to have no rules. The rules we make will have to be stronger than ever, but fair and open-minded, made by the majority for the majority. Those who don't wish to follow them will have to be educated with special care."

"Remember me."

"How could I ever forget you? I am so looking forward to seeing you at Seadrift!"

"I hope to be there."

Benedict and Mystica set off on the short walking route to Penvalley where they would collect the all terrain vehicle for the rest of the journey to Seadrift. They didn't notice that Philip had gone up to Edward with some urgency. He had been approached by one of the First City undercover workers.

"It's Kathleen," he said. "She's been taken for treatment."

"Kathleen? But what on earth happened?"

"Lucas saw her and had some notion of her from the past. He kept clawing at her and sobbing, saying 'Help' over and over. It's the only word he can say. He inadvertently betrayed her to Polly and Phoebe who were close by. They somehow put two and two together."
They had called the regulatory patrol officers who took Kathleen to the authority's questioning centre. This was obviously a real feather in their caps as it became clear that Kathleen was a strong member of an underground group to overthrow the regime."

"Shall I go and fetch Benedict and Mystica back?" asked Philip.

"No, no," said Edward. "There's nothing they can do. Let them go home. Things will be hot enough in due course and they could, like you, do with a bit of time to just be happy."

Ben and Mystica collected a vehicle from Ross at Penvalley and, as before, he had filled it with necessary provisions for their journey, and included a small bottle of champagne equivalent. News travels fast.

They took their time and travelled the hidden ways until they were well clear of First City.

"That was quite some visit," said Benedict. "I was so pleased to see Edward again; it's been quite a while, but he is looking more fragile than I would have hoped. I was delighted to meet Philip. What a true friend he will always be. And I was even more delighted to meet Lizzie and to see how much they suit each other!"

"Yes, I'm so glad they are such an obviously well-matched couple."

"Almost as well-matched as we are!"

"Benedict, I can't tell you how happy I am, how happy you have made me. I feel properly alive for the first time since I was a child. I now truly know how completely overwhelming love can be and I can't imagine life without you. I don't know what would have happened with Philip and me long term, but I suspect our love was destined to be a transitory thing, vital at the moment when we met and it first hit us."

"Well, you may be right. My only concern is that I will be worthy of your love and will be able to help you to sustain the happiness you feel now. I adore you and I know that, for me, life without you would not be any kind of life. I think that, after Ellie, I was just ticking over until I met you. Guy has very much taken to you as well, and I can see that he thinks the world of you."

"He's just the kind of son I would wish to have in an ideal world, so I will keep him as my own! I suppose I am allowed a small portion of regret that childbirth and the opportunity to bring up my own baby has been denied to me."

"You know, sometimes, just sometimes a sterilisation doesn't work properly. You never really had much of an opportunity to find out. In First City I know that many sterilisations were done hurriedly and yours may not have been done correctly. Also, some sterilisations can be reversed through fertility treatment. It's a bit of a long shot, but it's possible. And you are partnered with a doctor..."

"But I'm also nearly 40. I'm too old."

"Not a bit of it. You still have periods?"

"Yes, I do. Are you saying that it is just possible that I could conceive?"

"Well, it's not impossible. Let's not get too excited, but let's not give up on the idea either."

"Benedict, I can't think of anything more wonderful than you being the father to my child."

"And I would be uniquely privileged to have a baby with you."

They stayed in the woods overnight, sheltered by dark full-leafed trees, under a canopy of stars. They made love with a mixture of passion and extreme gentleness and Mystica had never felt so cherished.

The next morning they got up at the early signs of dawn breaking and continued to Seadrift, happy to see the first sight of the shoreline and the dunes, and to catch the cries of the seabirds as they wheeled and veered over the rocky outcrops and skimmed the waves. They were looking forward to seeing everyone and being able to let their love be recognised and supported officially. Mystica couldn't wait to receive the congratulations and to feel the warmth that she knew would be expressed.

They made their way first to Benedict's unit to see Guy and were surprised to find that he wasn't there. There was a note on the table. "Have gone to the Baxters'. Come as soon as you can." That sounded a bit abrupt, with a worrying note of some sort of warning. They made their way straight to the Baxters' unit and Joseph came out to greet them.

"Great to have you back, and we're so delighted for you that things can now carry on in the way we all knew was on the cards."

"What's happened, and where's Guy? Is he OK? Is everyone OK?"

"He's fine and everyone here is fine too. But we got a message through from Philip to say that Kathleen had been taken and treated.

They heard just as you were leaving, and of course Edward wouldn't allow anyone to fetch you back. He felt, and quite right too, that you both deserved some time to enjoy your happiness, before it was blighted in some way."

"Oh no!" said Mystica. "Kathleen was my line manager at the office and for a long time I thought she was ultra critical of me. She always seemed to be on my back, somewhat hostile, strict and hard-nosed, with no lightness to her at all. I then discovered that she was the very person who saved Philip and me from probably being taken and punished in some way. She had actually looked after my interests all the way along the line. How wrong I was. An incredible lady. I can't believe it. What happened?"

Joseph told them how, inadvertently, she had been betrayed by Lucas and then taken to the questioning area. Not his fault at all - he was so out of it that he had no idea what he was doing and left the way open for Polly to point the finger at Kathleen. But the authorities wasted no time and she was inflicted with nerve pain in order to get her to talk, to name names, to betray Edward and the other members working outside the community on Edward's behalf.

"Knowing Kathleen, they must have had an impossible task trying to get her to hand over information of any kind," said Benedict. "I remember her from way back. She's a wonderful lady, but austere and serious, not someone to provoke in any way. I can't imagine her divulging the least little bit of information that would be of any use to anybody."

"Well, that was the case. She had no intention of giving in. They tried their hardest in the most unpleasant ways possible, but gave up. She was treated and then thrown out on the streets. They watched her for a while in the hope that she would lead them to the community, but she appeared disorientated and it seemed as if she had lost her memory. I don't know how accurate that was. There was always more to Kathleen than met the eye."

The rest of the family came out, together with Guy, Samuel and Henny. They were all very subdued, although pleased to see

Benedict and Mystica, and Henny was the first to run over and give Mystica a hard squeeze.

"Isn't it just awful?" she said. "I never met Kathleen, but Samuel has told me about her and she is clearly one hell of a brave lady."

Samuel took up the story.

"Brooks kept a close eye out for her just in case, and late yesterday he saw her staggering through the streets, wandering round the edges of the community. He managed to take her into the unit. Fortunately Brooks is the master of covert activity, so he could manage this without being seen and he was able to take only the minimum risk with Kathleen."

"So, where is she and what's happening?" asked Mystica.

"She's very weak, but she's being nursed by Evelyn and Ava together, as far as their roles allow, work-wise inside the community. Lizzie is helping more with the nursery, so Evelyn has a freer hand and a bit more time. Some of the others are also helping, of course."

"I must go back," said Benedict. "See what I can do."

"Tomorrow," says Marnie. "You need a few hours rest first; otherwise you will be next to useless. Tomorrow."

"And I will come with you, of course," says Mystica. "I can take a share in the nursing."

Guy asked if he go with them. He wanted to meet Edward and also connect up with Philip. He was interested in Philip's background in design as he had some ideas for the immediate future at Seadrift and possible ways forward with other outlying communities. Benedict was pleased to have Guy's company with them and it seemed important that Guy should have the opportunity to meet Edward. Life was a precarious commodity when one got past a certain age and Edward was getting towards that time when the days would go quickly and the time remaining would be brief.

Samuel and Henny decided to stay a little longer to discuss farming issues with Joseph and Juno, and to meet others from the community to work out where each individual could make the most worthwhile contribution, according to his skills. They moved into the

Baxters' unit, which they knew would give Henny and Torrey more time on their own. With Joseph's help they made a list of the other outlying communities and the names and contact details of those who had any kind of leadership role.

Back at the First City community Benedict examined Kathleen carefully and tenderly. Edward was sitting by her side holding her hand and gazing into her eyes with a deep concentration, as if willing them to have some sort of bright response. He had the utmost gratitude to her for not betraying them and was desperate for her to know that.

Benedict knew there was nothing more that he could do from the medical perspective.

"The nerve drugs she was given were devastating and have caused permanent, irrevocable damage. I have to say I think that her time is limited, so it is important to make her as comfortable as possible. But, Edward, she knows you're here, and she is contented that she did a top job in keeping you all safe, I'm sure."

Mystica joined forces with Ava and Evelyn to nurse her. They washed her with warm scented water, soothing her frail skin, and kept a low gentle light in the room. Edward sat by her side day after day in the hope that there would be a glimmer of the old Kathleen about her, but she was unable to communicate at all and had slipped into unconsciousness.

Then one morning, when Ava went to check on her first thing she found Kathleen had died in the early hours.

Edward had been with her. He was devastated and went to his private garden to meditate and grieve.

Chapter 38   Guy and Edward

For a while Edward didn't feel up to talking to anyone much. Everyone felt they should respect this time he wanted on his own, until Guy decided that he needed to go and see Edward, to talk to him and find out some of his ideas for the future before time ran out. He didn't mention it to Benedict or Mystica, just made his way to Edward's quarters and knocked gently on the door. The opening mechanism was activated and Guy stepped in, somewhat cautiously.

He had not visited Edward's unit before. In fact he'd not really met Edward yet, just sort of seen him from a distance, but he felt it was time they did meet.

Edward was sitting by the side of his pool, watching the water as it cascaded from the fountain and streamed down the walls in a burst of artificial sunshine.

"That's amazing," said Guy. "Far better than the area we have at home."

Edward turned and smiled at Guy. "You're Benedict's son, Guy. Am I right?"

"Yes indeed, and I'm sorry to push in, but I really wanted to meet you and, well, to be frank, I felt you needed something, somebody to be here with you, however much you may have given the opposite impression. I think you have been on your own quite a while and it's time to be with people again. And I suppose I was also feeling a bit overeager to meet you. You're an important person in so many lives, you know, even for people like me who haven't met you."

"Sometimes the impatience of youth takes over in the most appropriate way," said Edward. "You're quite right. I think I do need somebody to be here, something to do. I have done my mourning and it's time to stir my stumps and get on with things. And I haven't welcomed you to our home. What a poor host!"

"Well, this has been a difficult time for you and you have had a lot to think about," said Guy. "I like to be busy too and I have some ideas for the future of Seadrift and the other communities that I'd really like to discuss with you. And that makes me wonder. The other outlying communities all have names like Waterfield, Birchwood, Becktown, Wellcombe and so on, but I wonder if this place has a name? I've never heard one."

"It should have, but it hasn't been considered really. I guess we've all been too busy just getting on with things. Perhaps that can be one of the first things you do - you could give a name to what I jokingly call The Fatherhouse. This place is the nearest I have ever come to having a home and a family for many years."

"I think that's exactly what it should be called, at least for now. It is hugely appropriate. I will spread the word. Your place here has always been that of a father figure and I think everyone thinks of you as someone they can come to for advice and help, perhaps to be directed and told off when necessary. By the way, I'm sorry if I have bothered you by being here."

Edward laughed.

"I'm so glad you came to see me. Thank you for 'bothering' me. I can see you are someone with perception. One day, in the not too distant future, there will be a major role for you in steering the direction of the new order. I already recognise in you the undeviating approach your mother used to take when she needed to talk to someone, and I'm also aware of the same element of compassion that she had for all her fellow human beings. She was a great lady, and if you exhibit even half of her wonderful consideration, you will have a lot to offer to people when the chips are down. And believe me, those testing times will come only too frequently in the days, months and years ahead."

"I wish so much that I had had time to know my mother."

"She will live again through you. This is the order of things. You have already made a start by coming to see me today. Who knows how long I might have just sat here contemplating my waterfall, if you hadn't dropped by? It is just exactly what she would have done."

"I just felt that you needed some company - it's a heavy load being a father figure. And I thought that, if you had really wanted to be on your own, you would have told me. In the nicest possible way!"

"You, Ben and Mystica will make a formidable trio and be a great team in the future."

"I'm so happy for Dad that Mystica came into our lives. He has so much needed someone like her, and she fills a big gap for me too."

"That's wonderful," said Edward.

"Can I come back and see you again soon?" asked Guy.

"I'd like nothing better," said Edward.

Mystica, Benedict and Guy made their plans to return to Seadrift once more. They were a bit taken aback to find that Guy had just gone to see Edward without talking it through first.

"I thought you would tell me to leave him alone," said Guy.

"Too right, I would have done," said Benedict.

"And you would have been wrong," said Mystica. "Guy has already shown that he has the skills to look at people and see what might make them happy, and healed in some way. He obviously struck exactly the right chord with Edward."

"Well yes," said Benedict, "and I would have just been doing the parental thing, trying to make sure that one's children don't interfere with other people and their lives. But I can see that you did Edward the world of good."

"He did me a lot of good too. It's one thing for *you* to say that I have characteristics of my mother in me, but it's quite different when that comes from someone like Edward. It's not that I don't believe you, but he could say that without bias of any kind, so it was even more powerful. I felt on cloud nine, wherever that might be. I asked if I could visit him at The Fatherhouse again."

"The Fatherhouse?" said Benedict and Mystica together.

"Yep, that's the name from now on for the First City Community. It needed a name and Edward and I came up with that between us, for the time being."

"Extraordinary," said Benedict. "You have never failed to amaze me."

"Well, I shall look forward to visiting again and talking to Philip as well about some design ideas for the other communities. I think they should all have the capacity for sunshine, for instance, real or artificial. The Fatherhouse should perhaps have a 'subtitle, something Latin, like Exumbris."

"My Latin is somewhat rusty."

"Ex umbris means out of the shadows," said Mystica. "My grandfather taught me Latin and I've never stopped being grateful. It's wonderful to know where our words come from, largely."

"Certainly, The Fatherhouse is a place that is out of the shadows and into the sunlight. So it's appropriate. We'll ask Edward if Brooks can let everyone know, via all communication channels to outlying communities, as well as the people who live in The Fatherhouse!"

Samuel and Henny returned to First City to report back to Edward and The Fatherhouse and to make arrangements for the next leg of their tour. They had secured the friendship of the Baxters, as well as many other new friends that even Mystica had yet to meet. Henny wanted Torrey to return to The Fatherhouse with them, but he was reluctant.

"Oh please," she said. "Ava will want to see you."

"Plenty of time," he said. "There's plenty of time and I have some musical work to do here."

He was also nervous about meeting up with his birth mother at this point and felt he needed time to get used to the changes in his life and what they might mean.

"OK," said Henny. "I understand. But don't leave it too long."

Chapter 39   Endings and beginnings

Guy and Mystica spent some time talking about the process of establishing a creativity base at Seadrift to begin with, to include fine arts, music, carpentry, theatre and home-making areas, plus a vital therapeutic unit. Benedict was the person with the greatest medical knowledge and so he would direct the therapeutic unit, together with Guy who had his mother's ability and interest in the ways in which people can be guided and supported through difficult times. It was acknowledged that there would be plenty of these ahead. The idea of a creativity base could then be duplicated in each of the outlying communities, with different focuses, depending on the skills of the individual residents.

Guy suggested that the development of architecture and engineering could be supervised and directed by Philip and Brooks in the Fatherhouse and Mystica was quick to agree.

It was good for Mystica and Guy to spend time together, away from Benedict. Time to get to know each other better, in the knowledge that they were almost family. They found they had both matching and complementary ideas.

"We need to see who else should be part of our creative team, here at Seadrift," said Mystica.

"For all her silliness, Susannah Templeton would be a good person to take on board. She needs something to do that stretches her imagination. She writes well, you know, and has sometimes come up with ingenious ideas. Her inventiveness could be harnessed I reckon. I guess it could also be the secret to opening her up to some of the more adult aspects of life."

"I'd go along with that, but maybe that's all part of her originality. I imagine she'll never really change!"

"Her parents are the teachers at Seadrift School. They teach everything, with the help of some historical online tutor programs, covering anything they feel unqualified to tackle. It has worked over the last few years, and there's always been something that has sparked an interest with all us kids."

"They sound just right. Torrey might want to come back here to The Fatherhouse, because of Henny and Ava. But if not, then we could certainly harness his unique musical talents at Seadrift."

"Well, I suppose it may not be easy for him to move away from everything he has ever known. The Baxters have always been his family and Henny and Ava are new in his life. I have no idea how it would work for me if I suddenly found I had a different father from the one I've always known. Of course, who knows? Perhaps I have..." He grinned and Mystica gave him a playful rap over the knuckles.

"I have another idea though, and I don't know how you feel about it, but I would be very keen to ask Philip to oversee the design part of any building work here at Seadrift, as well as directing architecture and building construction for all the communities, and perhaps Henny could look at the interior design. What do you think? Would it be awkward for you if Philip were involved?"

"Not one bit," said Mystica. "He and I have grown apart romantically but, strangely, much closer as good friends. I think it would be a wonderful idea, and I can't think of anyone better suited than Henny to look at interior design and probably run workshops. You know, I can't wait to get back to Seadrift and start putting some of these plans into action."

At that moment Samuel arrived in some distress.
"Where's Benedict? I thought he might be with you."
"He's taking some time in the nursery unit to check on the children's health. Do you need him?"
"It's Edward. Something's seriously wrong. I was with him and he seemed tired and a bit unfocused. And then suddenly he slumped over in his chair and he can't talk. Brooks is with him."
"I'll go and get Dad," said Guy.

Straight away Mystica went back with Samuel to Edward's quarters. She went to Edward and sat by his side.

"We're here Edward. You're alright. You're safe."

Brooks looked troubled.

"I can't mend him," he said. "I can't make it better."

Mystica stretched out her hand to Brooks and held on to him.

Benedict arrived and went to Edward. Edward was semi-conscious and unable to grasp Benedict's hand. His face was dragged down on one side and his left arm was useless.

"Edward, my dear friend, let's get you to bed," he said.

Brooks came forward and lifted Edward as easily as if he were a child, and carried him over to his bed. With great love and gentleness he undressed him and placed him under the coverlet. Edward exhaled and his eyes fluttered a little bit, before he lapsed again into unconsciousness.

"What's happened?" asked Samuel.

Benedict said "Edward has had a stroke. Samuel, you need to get the information out to everyone in The Fatherhouse. The next 48 hours are critical, and I would say that his life hangs in the balance. Samuel, you need to be prepared to take over from now on. If Edward makes a recovery it will not be complete and decision-making for the community is now, largely, in your hands."

"I'll go and let everyone know," said Samuel, visibly shaken by seeing his strong mentor changed into a shadow figure. He was aware, however, of where his duties now lay. With Henny at his side, they would need to make preparations for the future.

Mystica sat with Edward talking quietly to him all the time.

"Edward, my dear 'almost' grandfather, I love you with all my heart and I want to thank you for everything you have done for me and for those I cherish. You said to me just a little while ago 'Remember me'. And I think I said I will never forget you. None of us will. You are the reason that so many of us are here and ready to renew and regenerate First City and all its surroundings. And we will. We will all take it forward with you in our hearts."

She felt a slight squeeze of her hand and saw a faint lopsided smile on Edward's face.

"He squeezed my hand," she whispered to Benedict. "He's going to be fine. I'm sure he will."

Brooks said he wanted to adjust the lighting in Edward's room and needed to go back to his workshop for some tools.

As he left, Mystica stood up and went over to Benedict. She put her arms round him and whispered again to him.

"I have missed a period. My breasts feel tender and I was sick this morning. Do you think...?"

Benedict gave her a gentle hug. "Could well be. I guess your surgeon didn't do as good a job fixing you as he thought. And it's quite possible that your fallopian tubes have had time to grow back together. It happens. And if, a cautious if, you are pregnant then I can't think of anything more wonderful."

"I want to tell Edward. I think he would be pleased and it will give him something to look forward to."

Benedict smiled and nodded, as Mystica went back to sit with Edward.

"Edward, Benedict and I want you to be the first to know that we are pretty sure we have a baby on the way. There will be a newcomer at Seadrift and I look forward to bringing him, or her, to meet one of the most wonderful people I have ever known. Be pleased for us!"

Edward tried hard to smile again, but the effort was too great.

"I think you should leave him now to have a rest. I will stay and I will send for you and Samuel if there are any changes."

Benedict hoped that he could do something to aid Edward's recovery. He hated the idea that he needed to prepare Mystica for the end but the signs were not good.

After watching over Edward for some time, Benedict dropped off to sleep in Edward's chair and woke with a start. He immediately checked for vital signs, but it was all too clear that Edward had drifted off in his sleep and died peacefully. He sat on his own with the man, remembering the great feeling of peace and calm that he had always felt whenever he attended the death of a patient. It was a privilege, he felt, to share the extraordinary seconds when the body was honoured by a certain dignity, even if the final moments had been crushing. He never really wanted to share this short time. It was his and his alone. He then stirred himself and contacted Mystica and Samuel.

Benedict, Guy and Mystica stayed in The Fatherhouse for a few weeks, spending time with everyone, talking about the wonderful times they had spent with Edward, and talking about the wonderful person he had been. It was a time for reflection, for sadness and for discussions about moving on.

It was clear that Mystica's pregnancy symptoms were real and she was sicker in the early days than she'd ever been in her life.

"If only I'd known!" she said. "This is dreadful" and she dashed yet again to the bathroom and existed on weak tea and water biscuits.

Lizzie laughed and teased her, saying "It gets worse. Your bladder won't obey you, you won't be able to pick anything up from the floor and your back will ache and keep you awake at night. Other than that I guess it's all plain sailing!."

Mystica, Benedict and Guy got ready to return to Seadrift. Lizzie was getting close to giving birth and Mystica promised to try and get back as soon as possible, if not for the birth itself. Evelyn had taken it upon herself to be the designated midwife and Lizzie was delighted.

Lizzie and Philip came, with Louis, to see them off on the journey home. Samuel and Henny had already said their goodbyes as they were both concentrating hard on the administration of The Fatherhouse and the outlying communities. Brooks and Ava came very briefly to say goodbye.

"Must get back," said Brooks. "Things to do! Help my wife." He gave Ava a hug, surprising them all, and then came forward and held Mystica close.

"Go well," he said. "Be happy and always be the person you are, a special friend."

Just as they were leaving, Philip called out to Mystica.
"Whoa, I nearly forgot! For you. Keep it safe!"
He kissed her and passed over a little package. She unwrapped it and there inside was the snow globe with her beloved Tiger, playing his saxophone in the middle of the swirling snowstorm.

"Perfect!" she said. "Thank you. Just perfect."

Milton Keynes UK
Ingram Content Group UK Ltd.
UKHW012002020524
442050UK00004B/240